MARWE

INTO THE LAND OF THE DEAD

AN EAST AFRICAN LEGEND

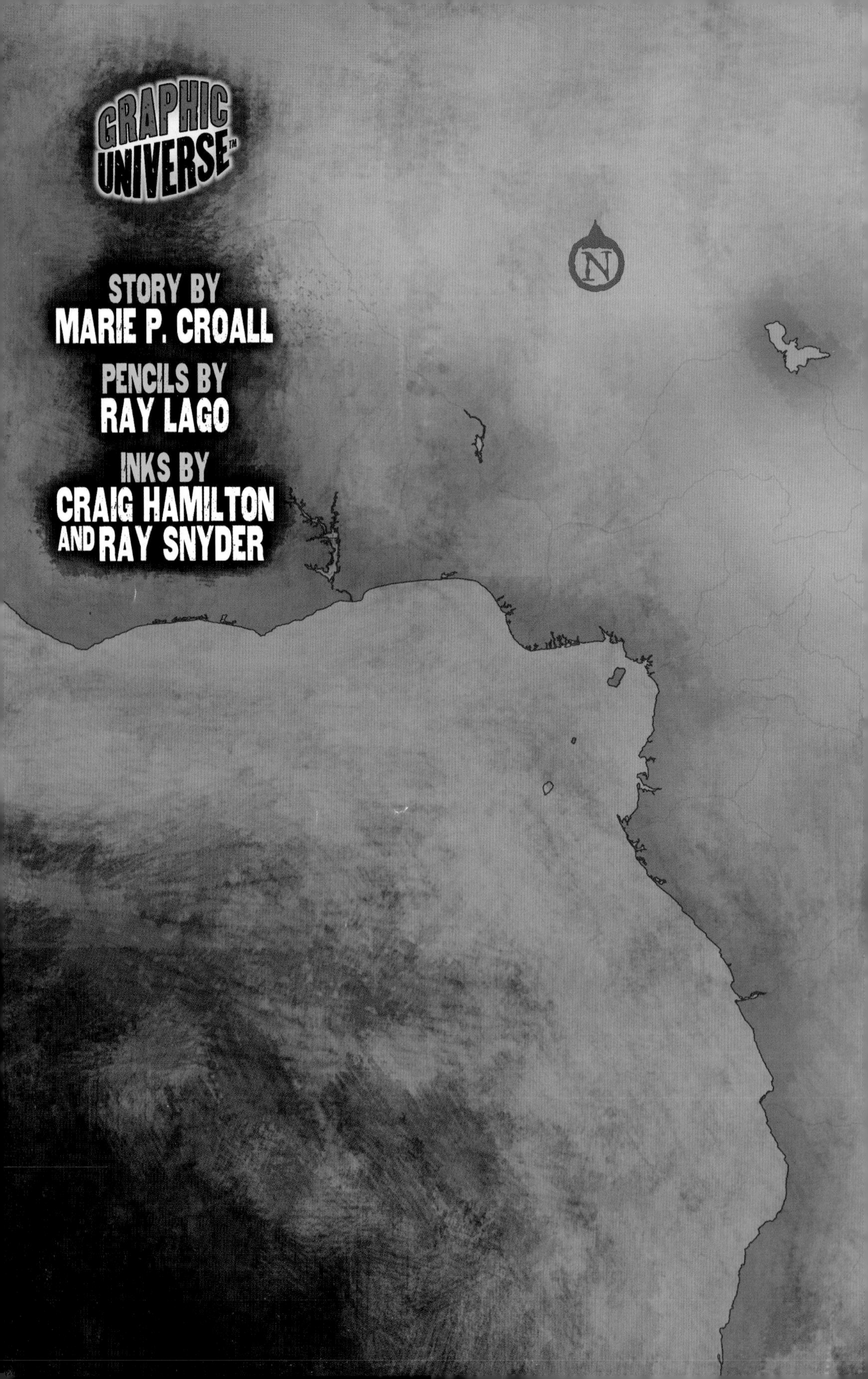
N

GRAPHIC UNIVERSE™

STORY BY
MARIE P. CROALL
PENCILS BY
RAY LAGO
INKS BY
CRAIG HAMILTON
AND RAY SNYDER

MARWE

INTO THE LAND OF THE DEAD

AN EAST AFRICAN LEGEND

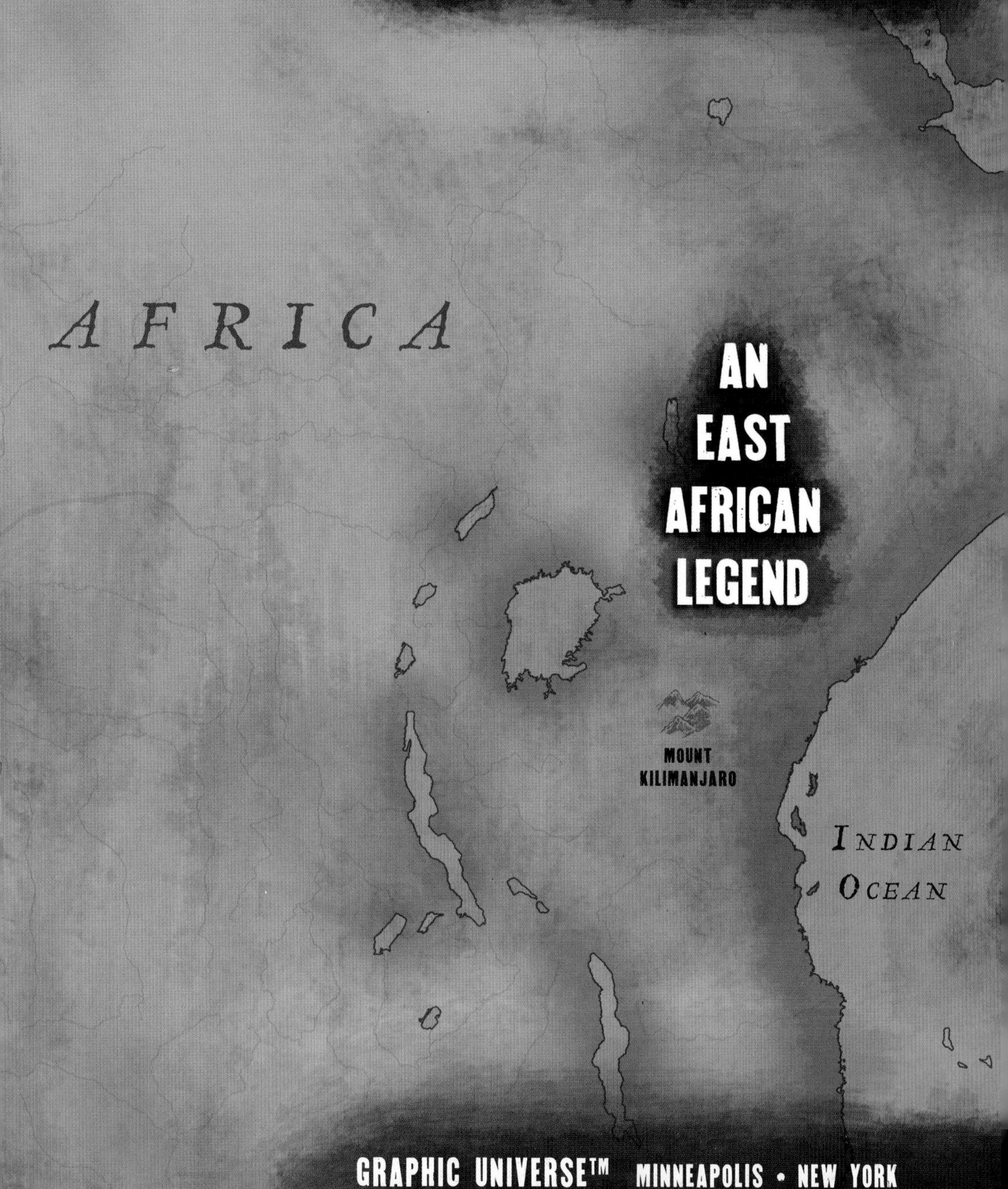
AFRICA
MOUNT KILIMANJARO
INDIAN OCEAN

GRAPHIC UNIVERSE™ MINNEAPOLIS • NEW YORK

Marwe is a tale from the Chaga, a Bantu-speaking people who have lived in East Africa for nearly a thousand years. Its origins are in the foothills of Mount Kilimanjaro, the tallest mountain in Africa, in what later became the country of Tanzania. Chaga legends and folktales have been passed down over the centuries by word of mouth and are seldom seen in print. Many of the stories address a young person's passage into adulthood, and one of the most famous is Marwe's trip to the Land of the Dead. Harold E. Scheub, professor of African Languages and Literature at the University of Wisconsin–Madison, reviewed Marie P. Croall's adaptation and Ray Lago's meticulous sketches to ensure faithfulness to the cultures and traditions of the peoples of East Africa.

STORY BY MARIE P. CROALL

PENCILS BY RAY LAGO

INKS BY CRAIG HAMILTON & RAY SNYDER

COLORING BY HI-FI DESIGN

LETTERING BY MARSHALL DILLON AND TERRI DELGADO

CONSULTANT: HAROLD E. SCHEUB, UNIVERSITY OF WISCONSIN–MADISON

Copyright © 2009 by Lerner Publishing Group, Inc.

Graphic Universe™ is a trademark of Lerner Publishing Group, Inc.

Graphic Universe™
A division of Lerner Publishing Group, Inc.
241 First Avenue North
Minneapolis, MN 55401 U.S.A.

Website address: www.lernerbooks.com

Library of Congress Cataloging-in-Publication Data

Croall, Marie P.
    Marwe : into the land of the dead : an east African legend / story by Marie P. Croall ; pencils by Ray Lago ; inks by Craig Hamilton.
        p.   cm. — (Graphic myths and legends)
    Includes index.
    ISBN: 978-0-8225-7134-6 (lib. bdg. : alk. paper)
    1. Chaga (African people)—Folklore. 2. Death—Folklore. 3. Graphic novels. I. Lago, Ray. II. Hamilton, Craig. III. Title.
GR356.72.C45C76 2009
398.2'08996395—dc22   2007001828

Manufactured in the United States of America
2 3 4 5 6 7 - DP - 14 13 12 11 10 09

TABLE OF CONTENTS

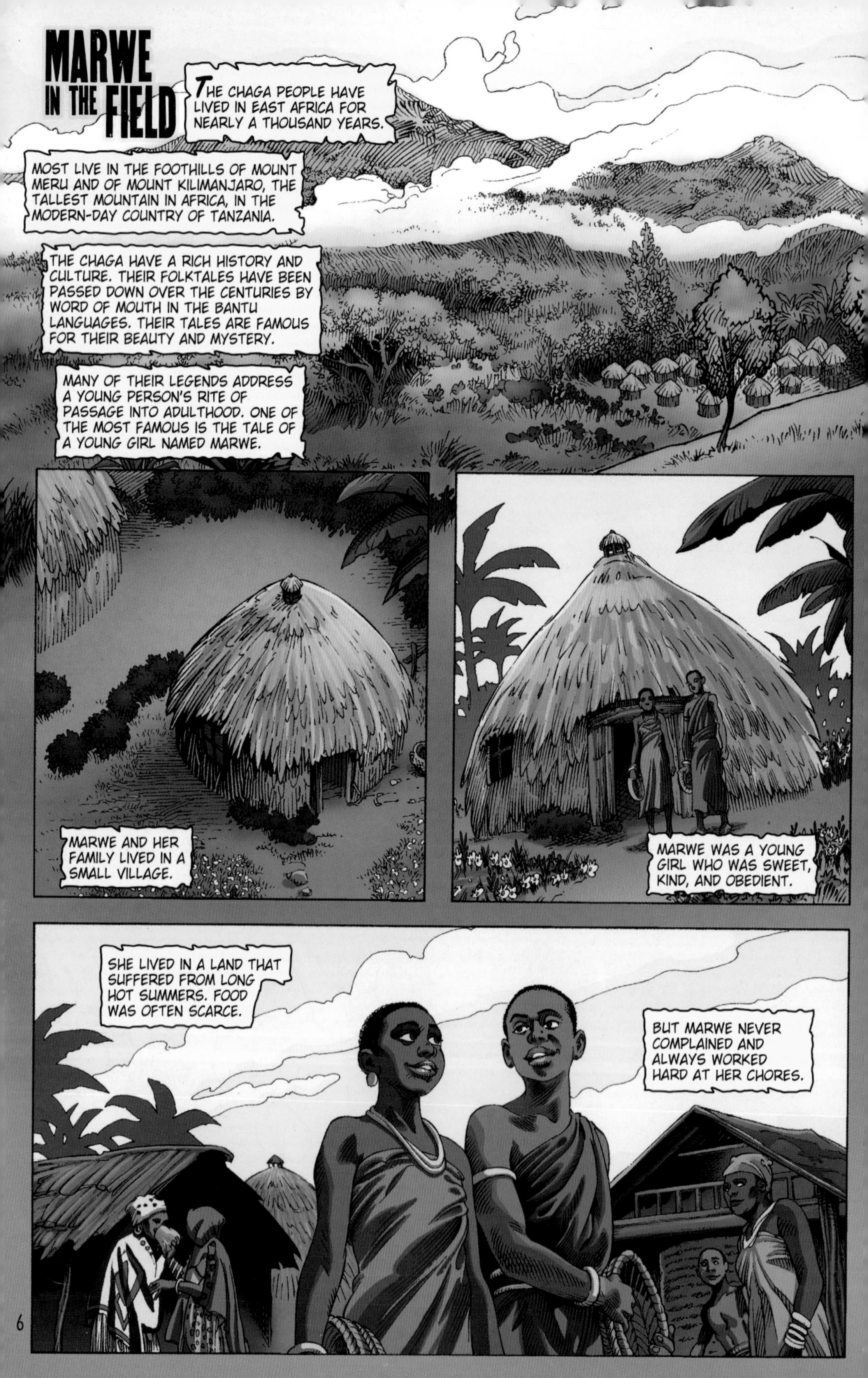
MARWE IN THE FIELD
THE CHAGA PEOPLE HAVE LIVED IN EAST AFRICA FOR NEARLY A THOUSAND YEARS.
MOST LIVE IN THE FOOTHILLS OF MOUNT MERU AND OF MOUNT KILIMANJARO, THE TALLEST MOUNTAIN IN AFRICA, IN THE MODERN-DAY COUNTRY OF TANZANIA.
THE CHAGA HAVE A RICH HISTORY AND CULTURE. THEIR FOLKTALES HAVE BEEN PASSED DOWN OVER THE CENTURIES BY WORD OF MOUTH IN THE BANTU LANGUAGES. THEIR TALES ARE FAMOUS FOR THEIR BEAUTY AND MYSTERY.
MANY OF THEIR LEGENDS ADDRESS A YOUNG PERSON'S RITE OF PASSAGE INTO ADULTHOOD. ONE OF THE MOST FAMOUS IS THE TALE OF A YOUNG GIRL NAMED MARWE.
MARWE AND HER FAMILY LIVED IN A SMALL VILLAGE.
MARWE WAS A YOUNG GIRL WHO WAS SWEET, KIND, AND OBEDIENT.
SHE LIVED IN A LAND THAT SUFFERED FROM LONG HOT SUMMERS. FOOD WAS OFTEN SCARCE.
BUT MARWE NEVER COMPLAINED AND ALWAYS WORKED HARD AT HER CHORES.

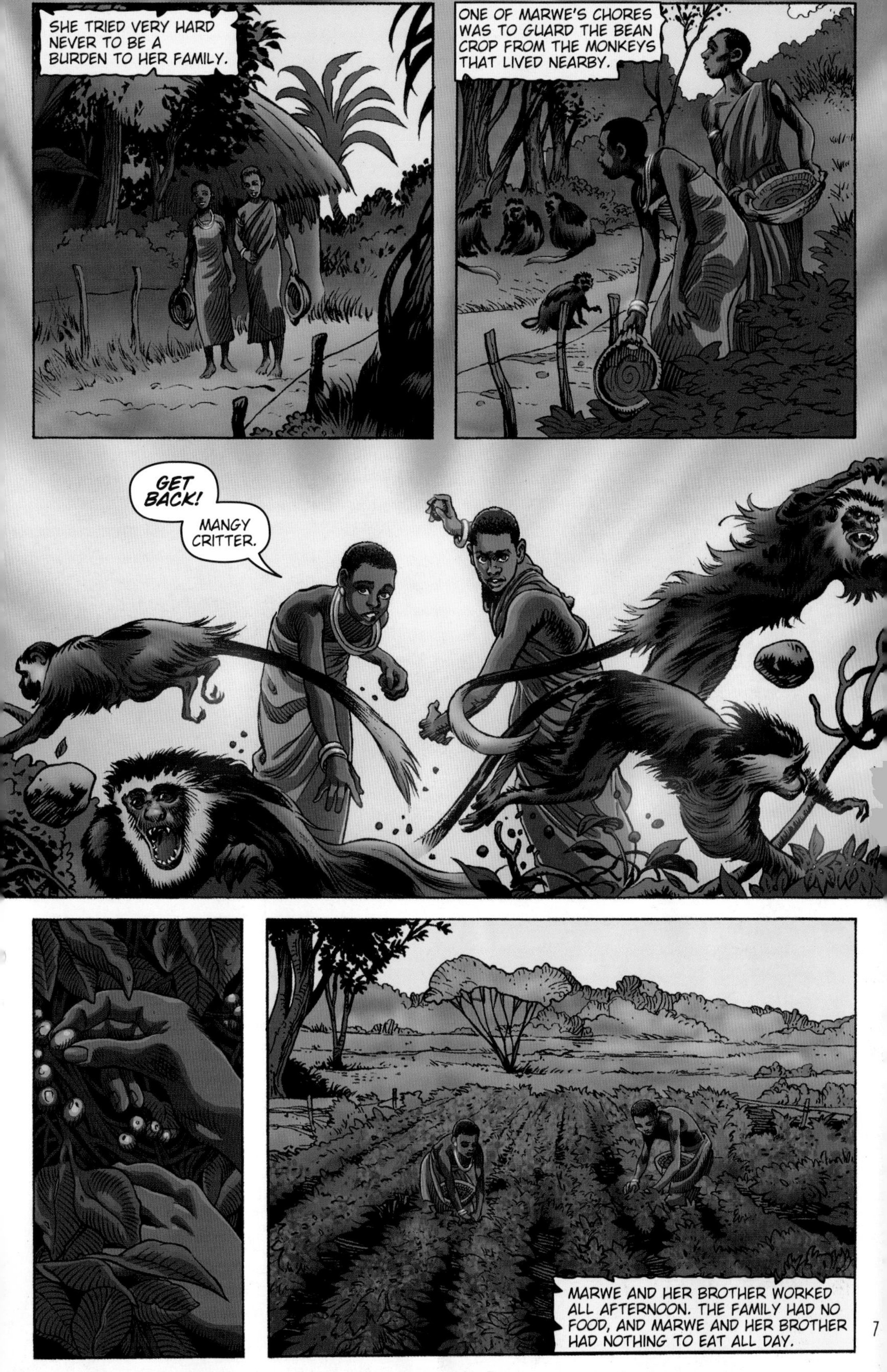
SHE TRIED VERY HARD NEVER TO BE A BURDEN TO HER FAMILY.
ONE OF MARWE'S CHORES WAS TO GUARD THE BEAN CROP FROM THE MONKEYS THAT LIVED NEARBY.
GET BACK!
MANGY CRITTER.
MARWE AND HER BROTHER WORKED ALL AFTERNOON. THE FAMILY HAD NO FOOD, AND MARWE AND HER BROTHER HAD NOTHING TO EAT ALL DAY.

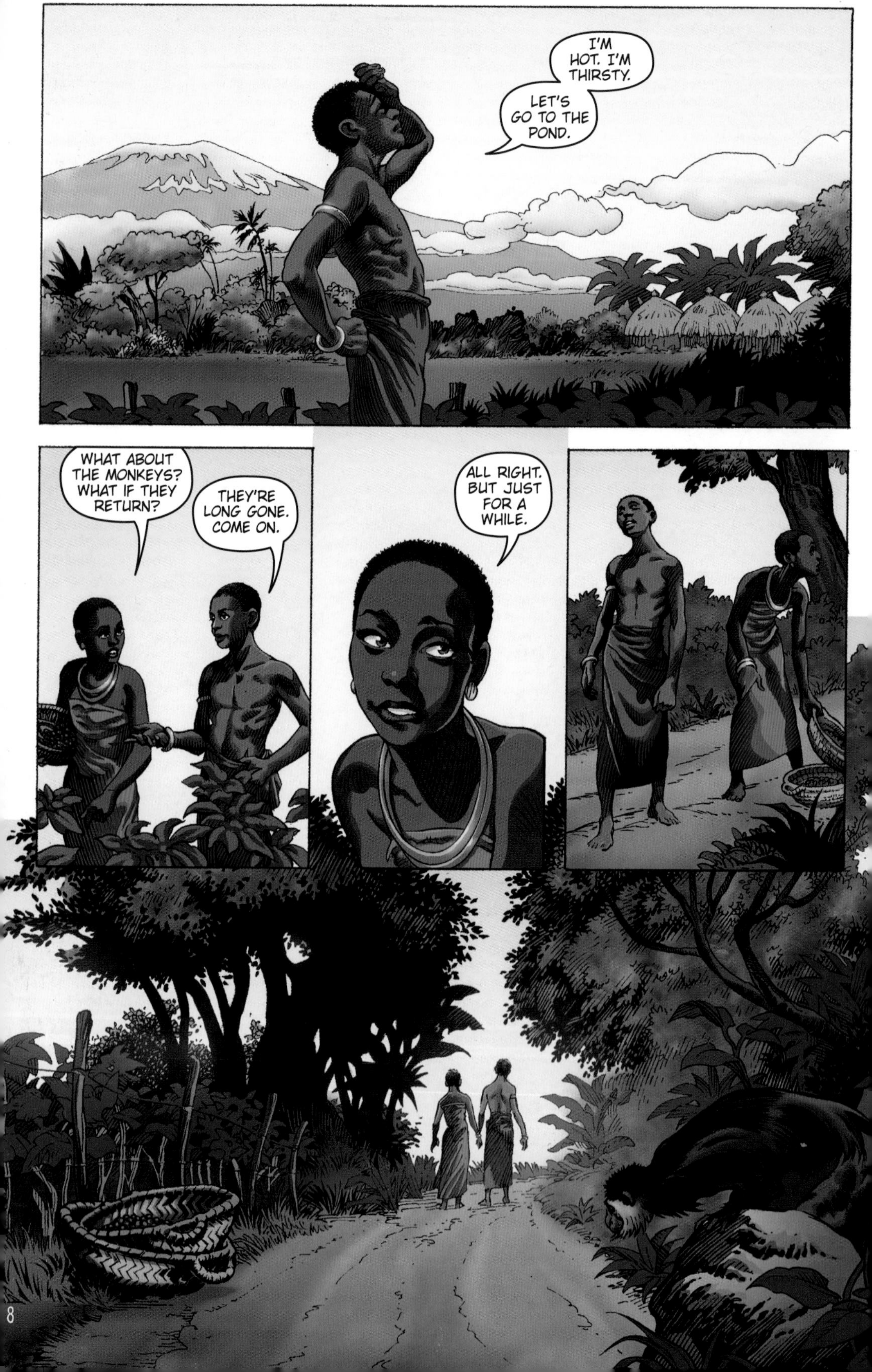
I'M HOT. I'M THIRSTY.
LET'S GO TO THE POND.
WHAT ABOUT THE MONKEYS? WHAT IF THEY RETURN?
THEY'RE LONG GONE. COME ON.
ALL RIGHT. BUT JUST FOR A WHILE.

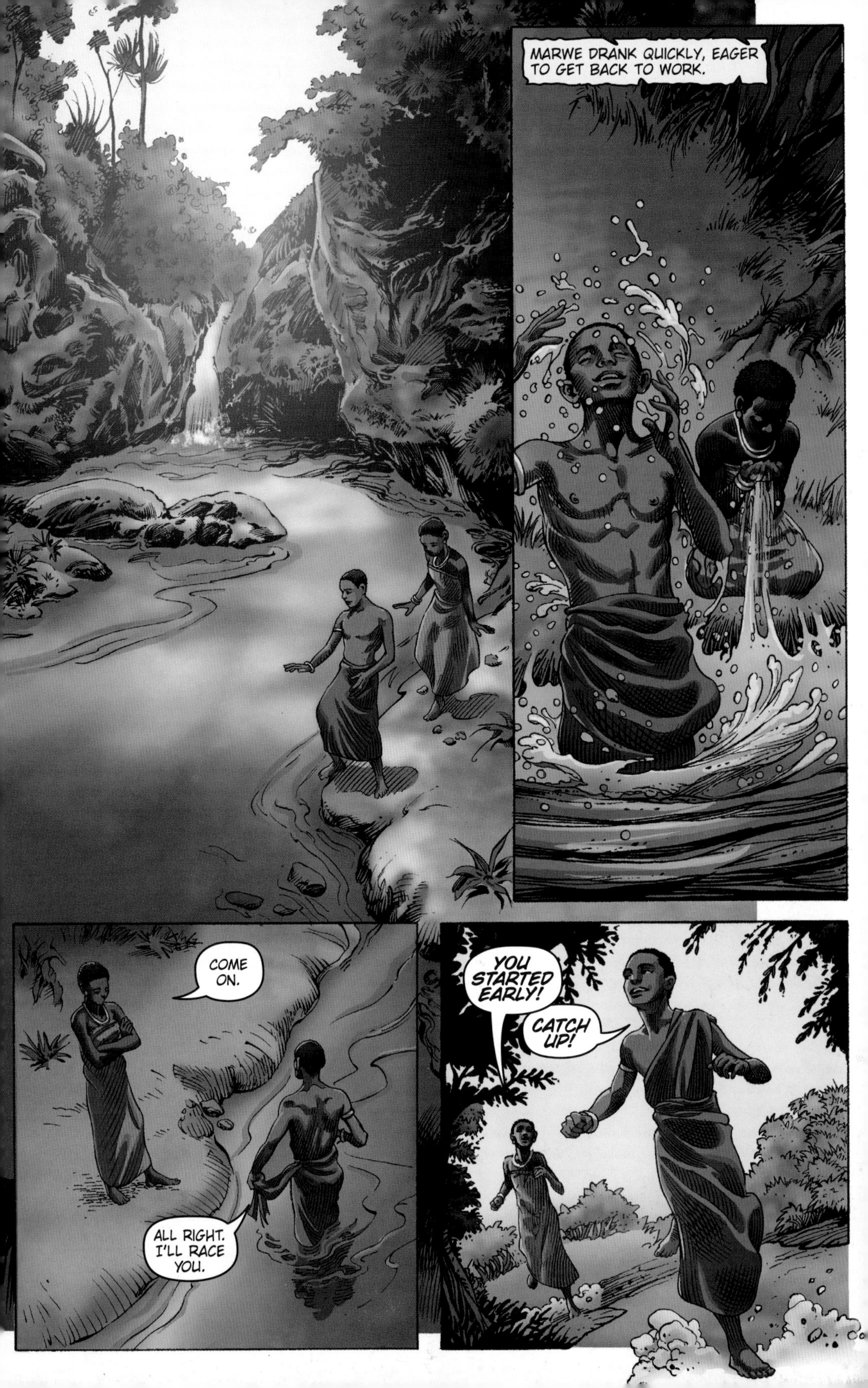
MARWE DRANK QUICKLY, EAGER TO GET BACK TO WORK.
COME ON.
ALL RIGHT. I'LL RACE YOU.
YOU STARTED EARLY!
CATCH UP!

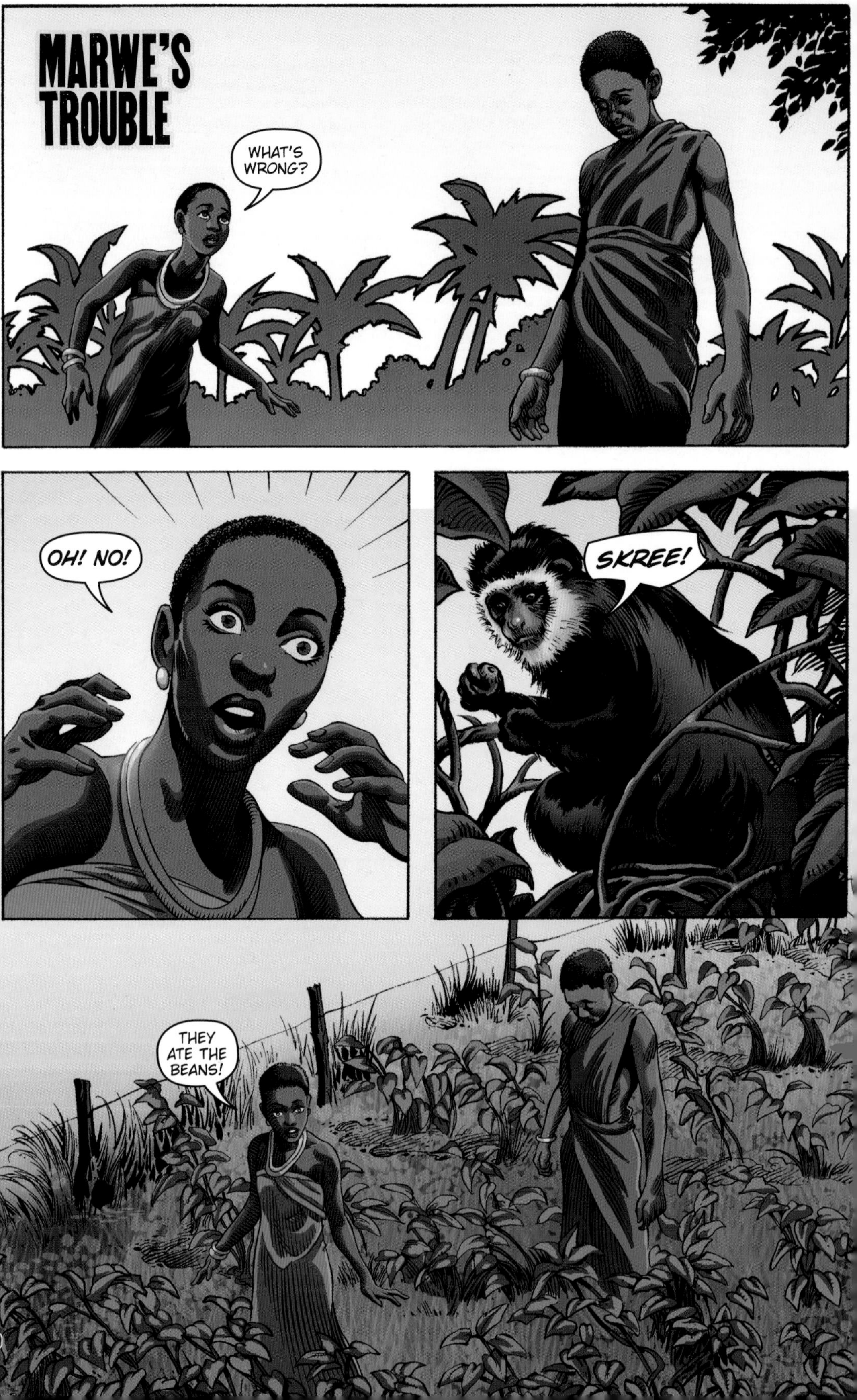
MARWE'S TROUBLE
WHAT'S WRONG?
OH! NO!
SKREE!
THEY ATE THE BEANS!

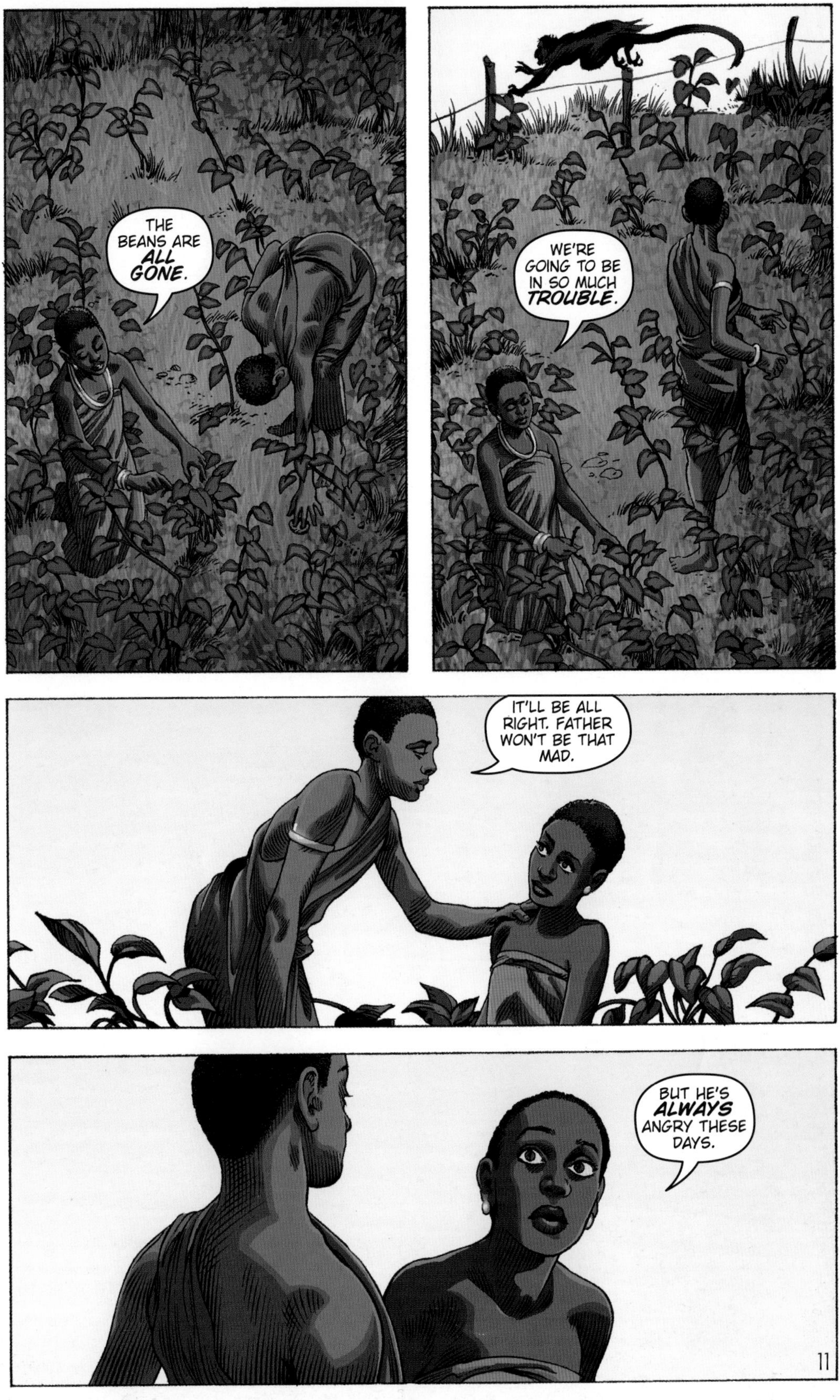
THE BEANS ARE ALL GONE.
WE'RE GOING TO BE IN SO MUCH TROUBLE.
IT'LL BE ALL RIGHT. FATHER WON'T BE THAT MAD.
BUT HE'S ALWAYS ANGRY THESE DAYS.

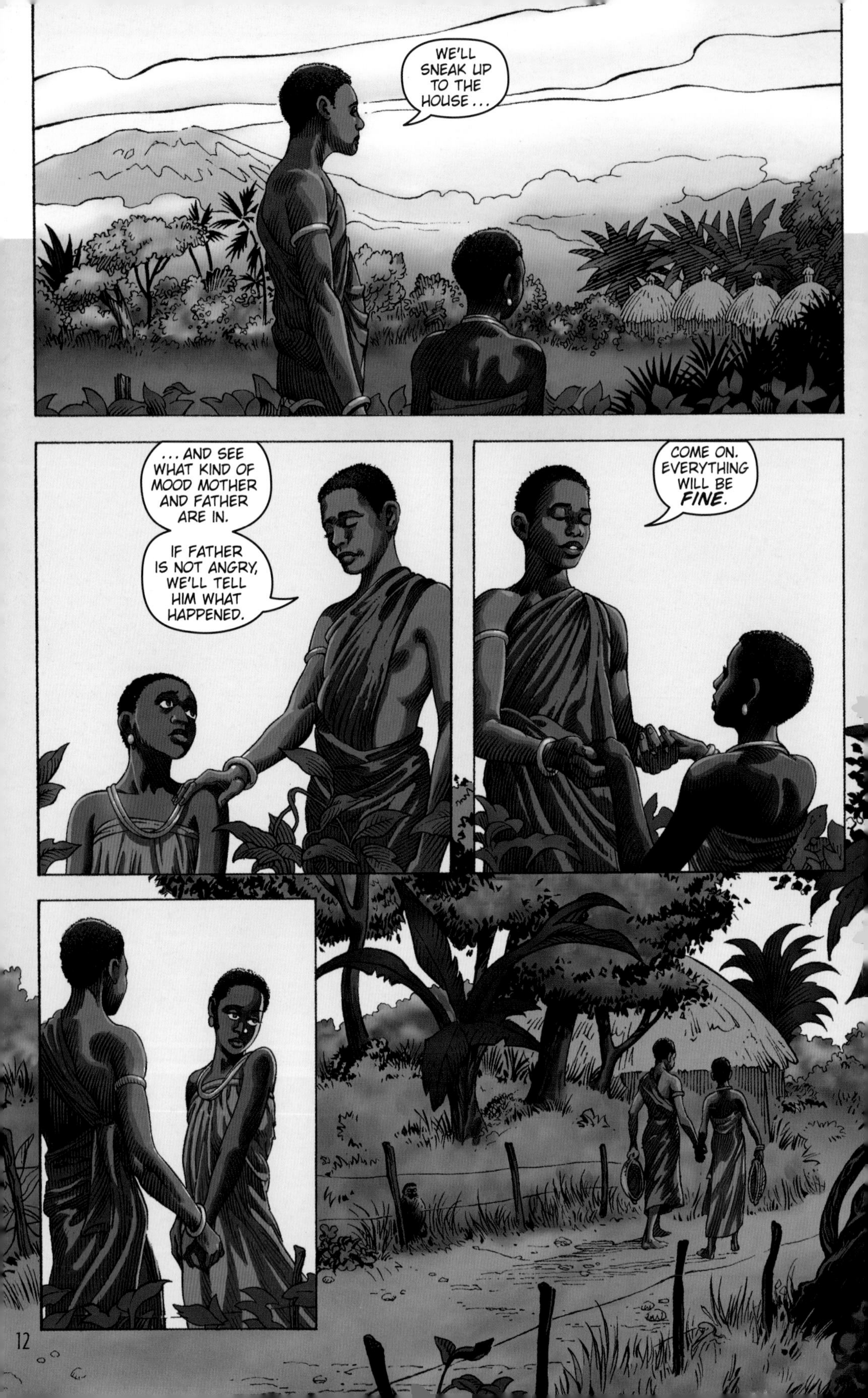
WE'LL SNEAK UP TO THE HOUSE . . .
. . . AND SEE WHAT KIND OF MOOD MOTHER AND FATHER ARE IN.
IF FATHER IS NOT ANGRY, WE'LL TELL HIM WHAT HAPPENED.
COME ON. EVERYTHING WILL BE *FINE*.

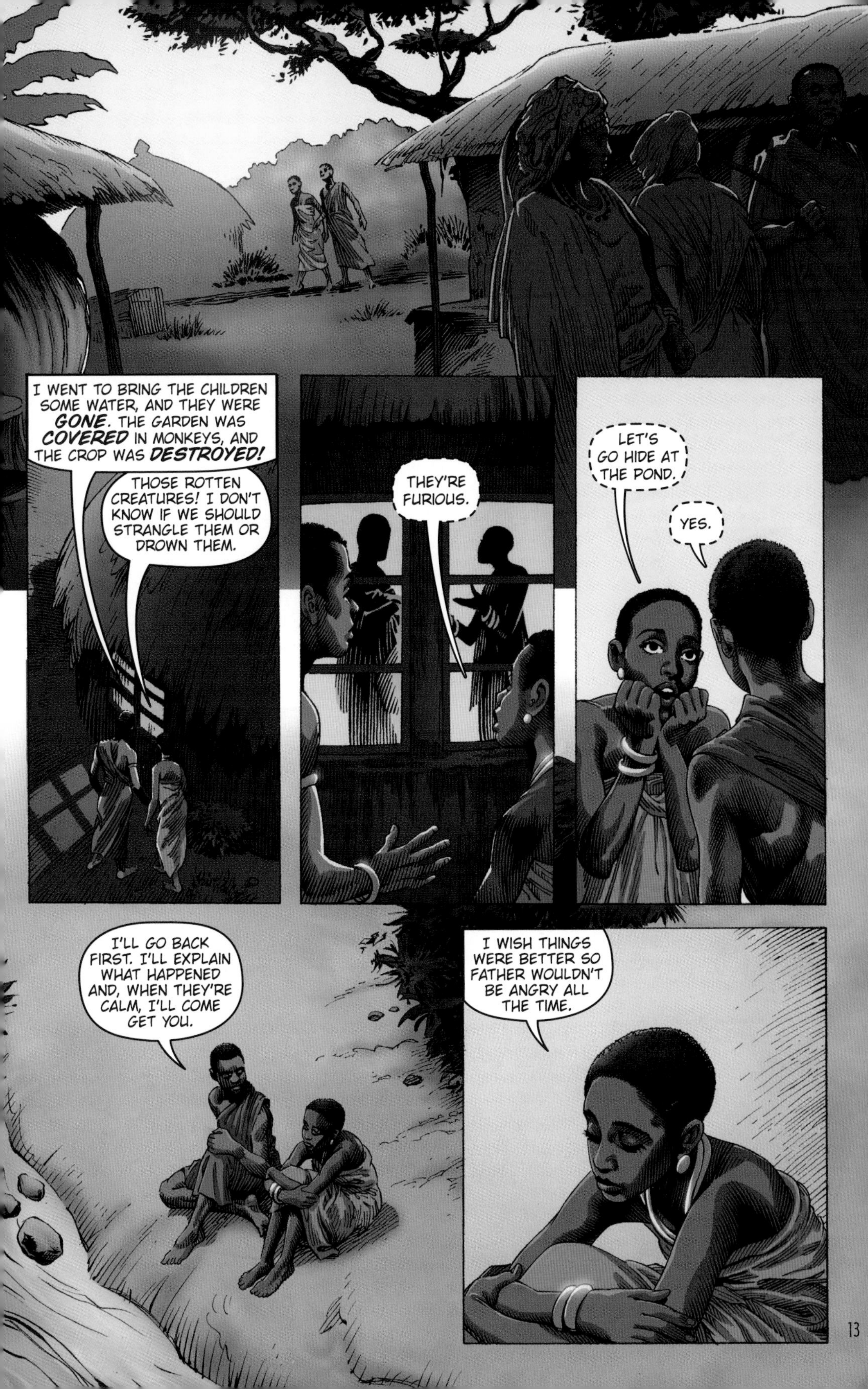

I WENT TO BRING THE CHILDREN SOME WATER, AND THEY WERE **GONE**. THE GARDEN WAS **COVERED** IN MONKEYS, AND THE CROP WAS **DESTROYED!**
THOSE ROTTEN CREATURES! I DON'T KNOW IF WE SHOULD STRANGLE THEM OR DROWN THEM.
THEY'RE FURIOUS.
LET'S GO HIDE AT THE POND.
YES.
I'LL GO BACK FIRST. I'LL EXPLAIN WHAT HAPPENED AND, WHEN THEY'RE CALM, I'LL COME GET YOU.
I WISH THINGS WERE BETTER SO FATHER WOULDN'T BE ANGRY ALL THE TIME.

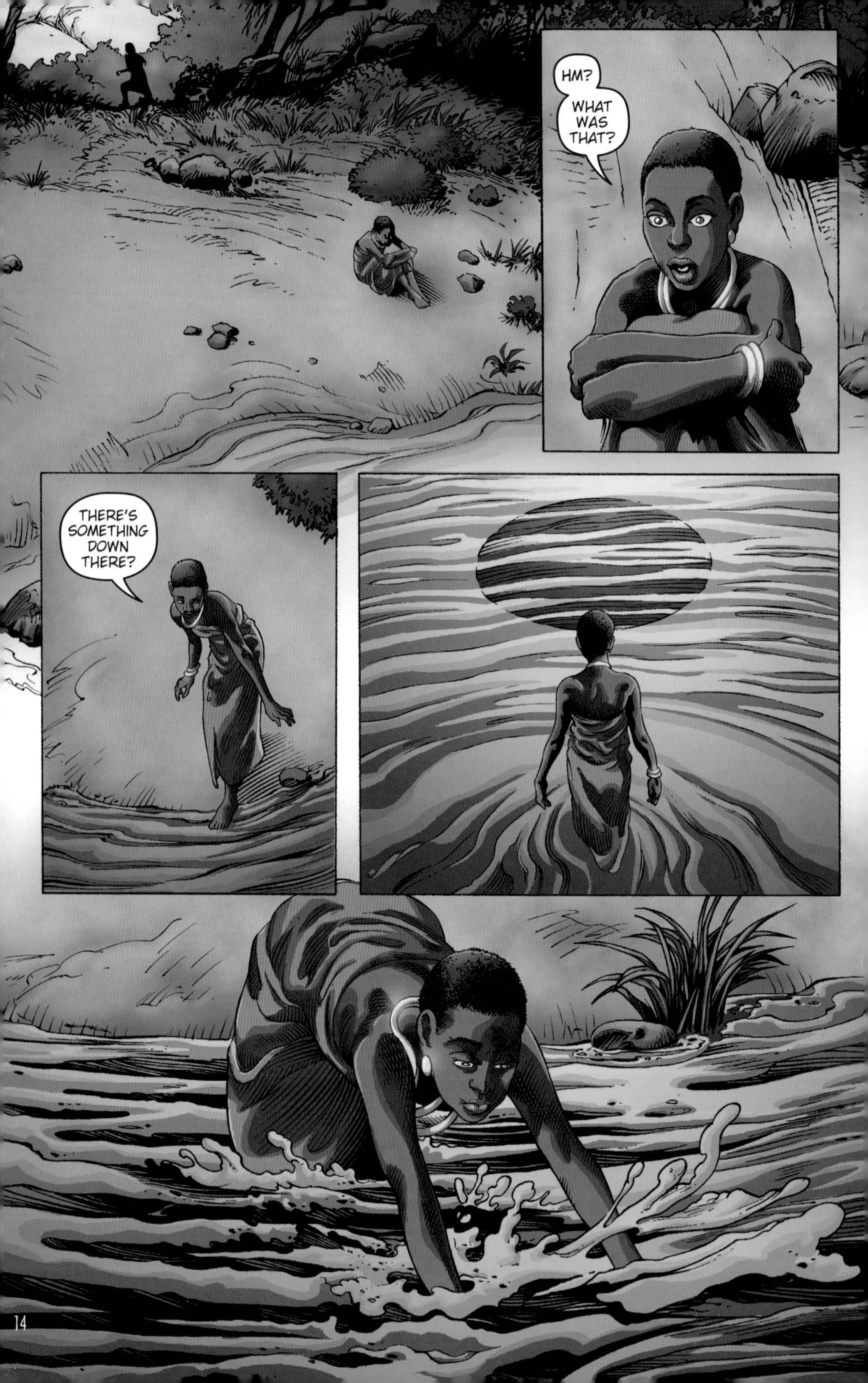
HM?
WHAT WAS THAT?
THERE'S SOMETHING DOWN THERE?

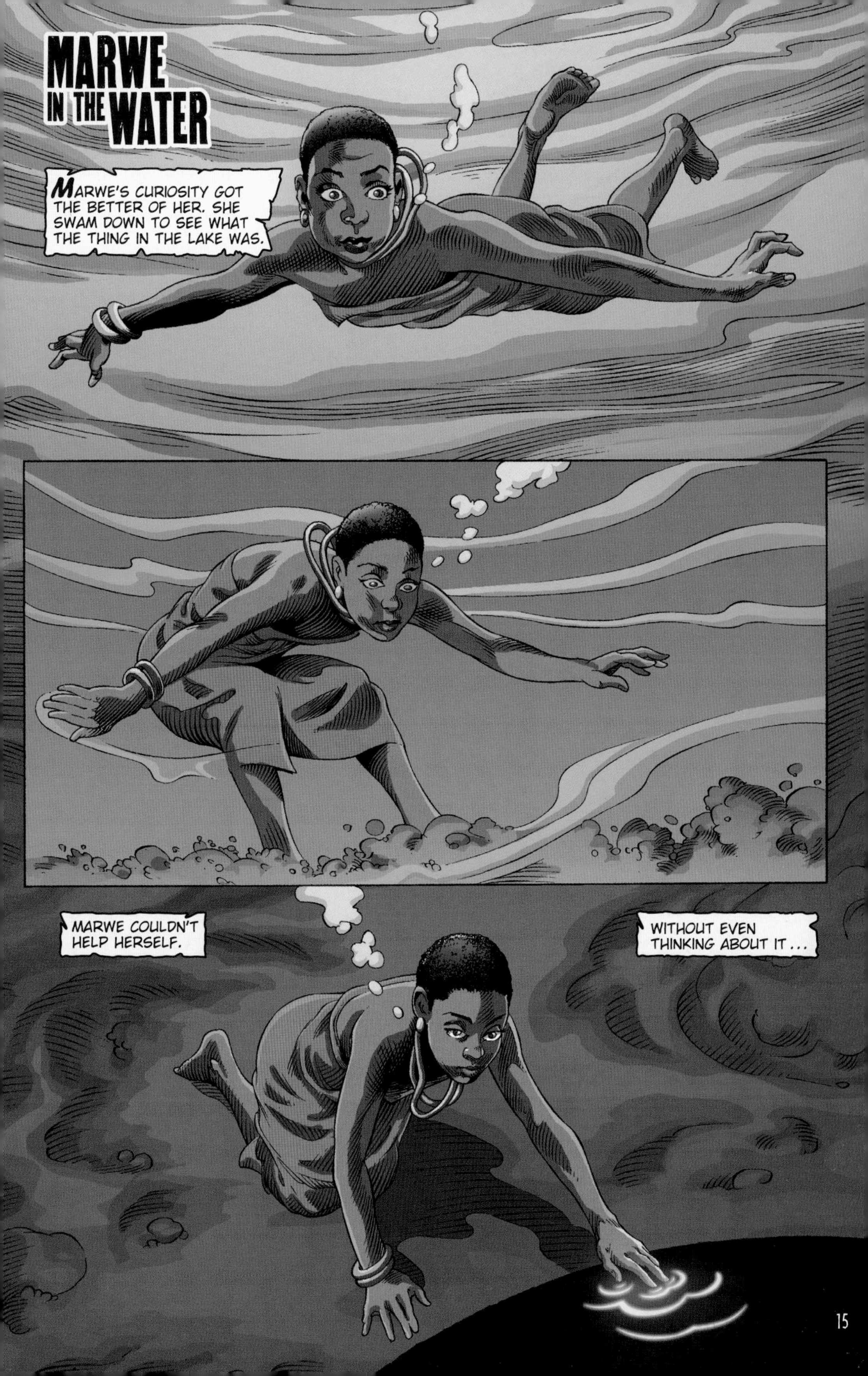
MARWE IN THE WATER
MARWE'S CURIOSITY GOT THE BETTER OF HER. SHE SWAM DOWN TO SEE WHAT THE THING IN THE LAKE WAS.
MARWE COULDN'T HELP HERSELF.
WITHOUT EVEN THINKING ABOUT IT . . .

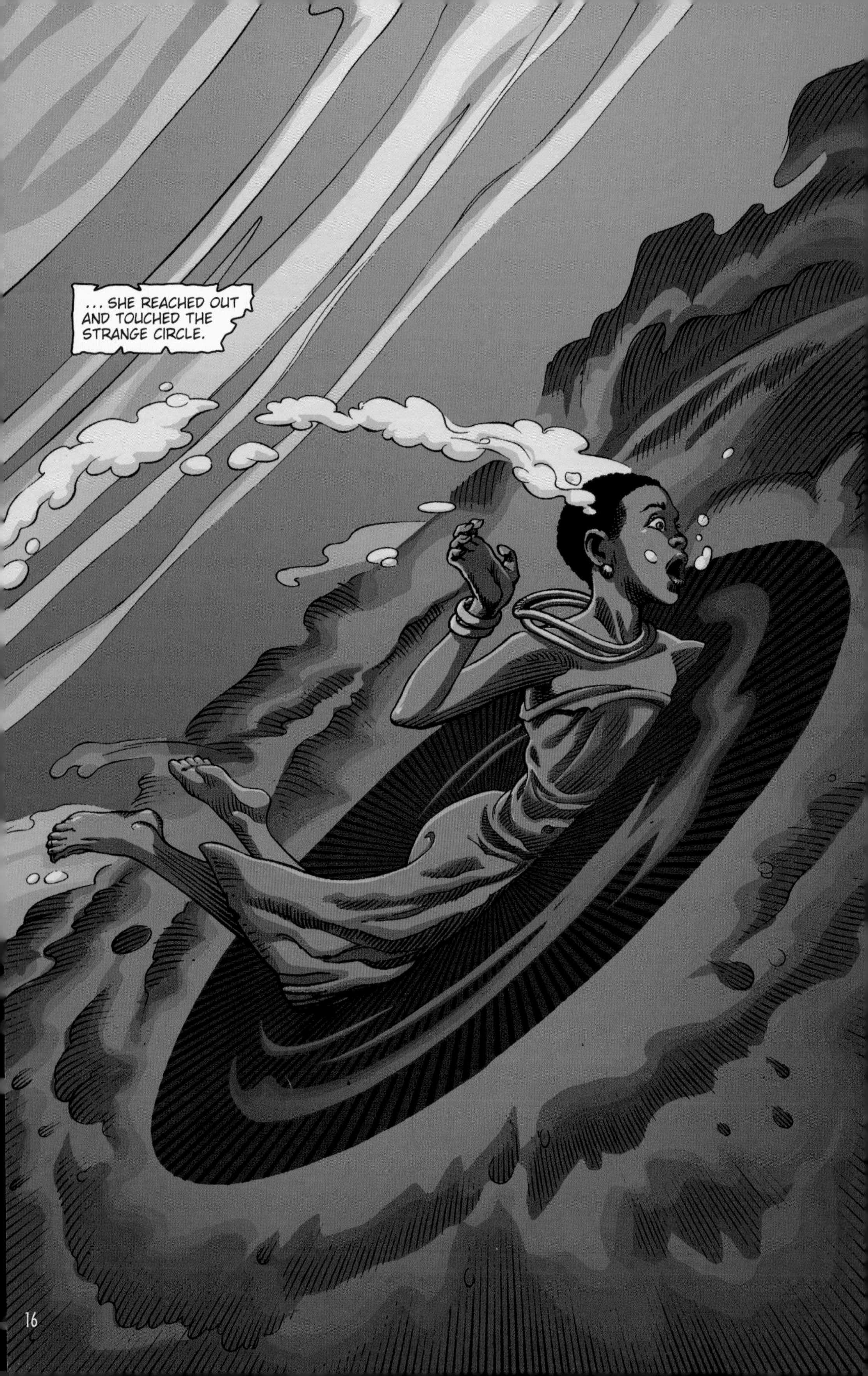
... SHE REACHED OUT AND TOUCHED THE STRANGE CIRCLE.

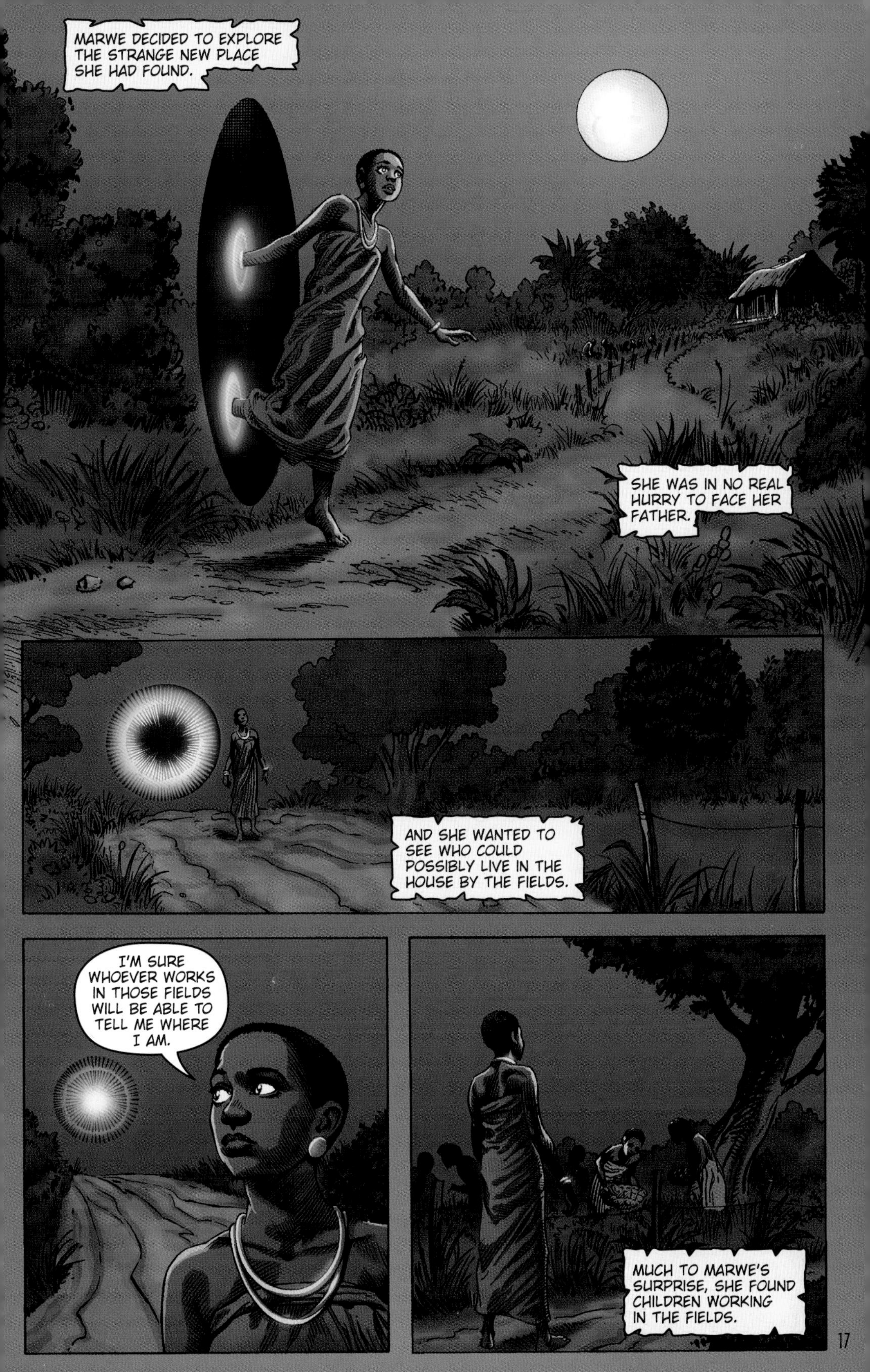
MARWE DECIDED TO EXPLORE THE STRANGE NEW PLACE SHE HAD FOUND.
SHE WAS IN NO REAL HURRY TO FACE HER FATHER.
AND SHE WANTED TO SEE WHO COULD POSSIBLY LIVE IN THE HOUSE BY THE FIELDS.
I'M SURE WHOEVER WORKS IN THOSE FIELDS WILL BE ABLE TO TELL ME WHERE I AM.
MUCH TO MARWE'S SURPRISE, SHE FOUND CHILDREN WORKING IN THE FIELDS.

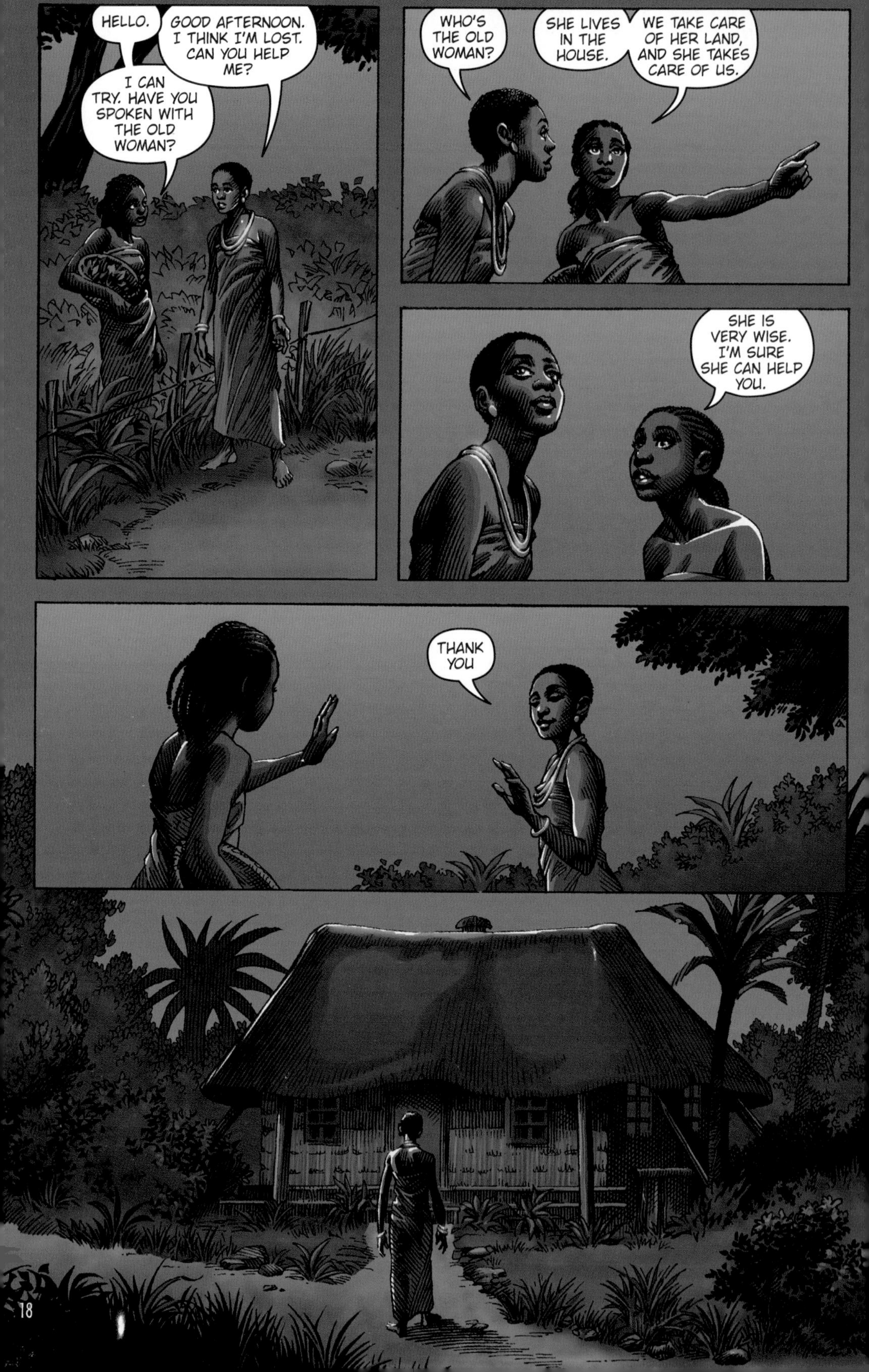
HELLO.
GOOD AFTERNOON. I THINK I'M LOST. CAN YOU HELP ME?
I CAN TRY. HAVE YOU SPOKEN WITH THE OLD WOMAN?
WHO'S THE OLD WOMAN?
SHE LIVES IN THE HOUSE.
WE TAKE CARE OF HER LAND, AND SHE TAKES CARE OF US.
SHE IS VERY WISE. I'M SURE SHE CAN HELP YOU.
THANK YOU

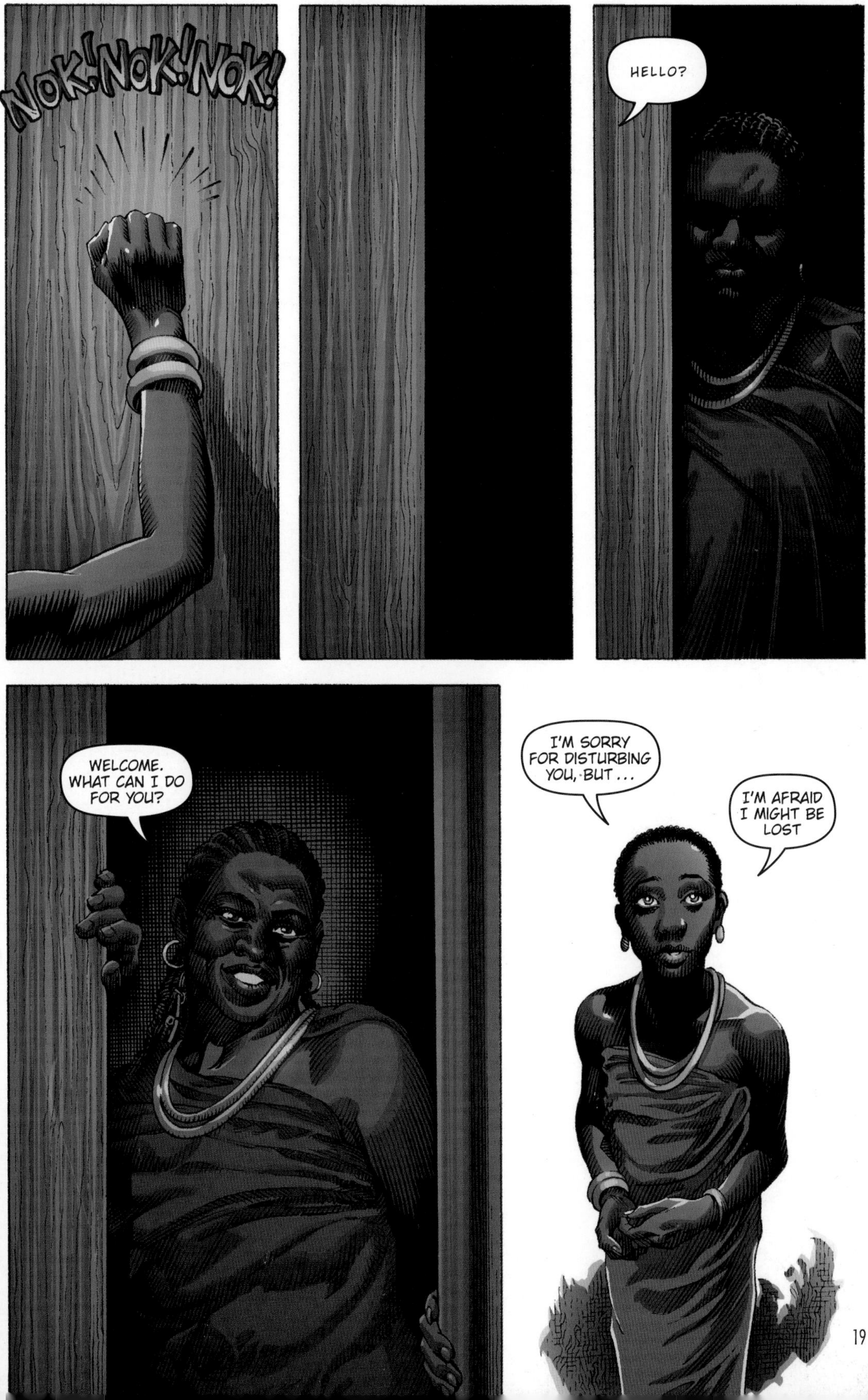
NOK! NOK! NOK!
HELLO?
WELCOME. WHAT CAN I DO FOR YOU?
I'M SORRY FOR DISTURBING YOU, BUT . . .
I'M AFRAID I MIGHT BE LOST

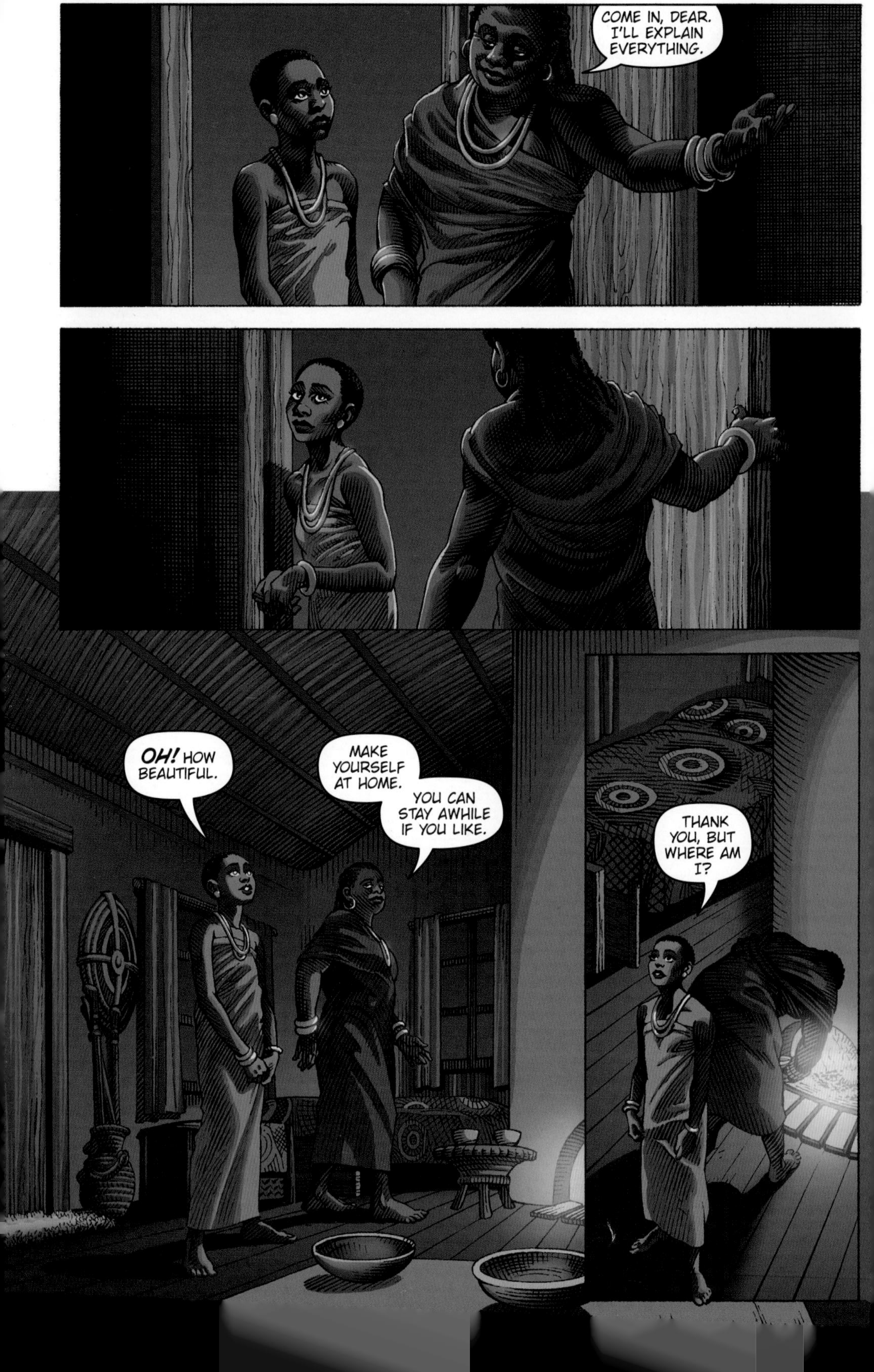
COME IN, DEAR. I'LL EXPLAIN EVERYTHING.
OH! HOW BEAUTIFUL.
MAKE YOURSELF AT HOME.
YOU CAN STAY AWHILE IF YOU LIKE.
THANK YOU, BUT WHERE AM I?

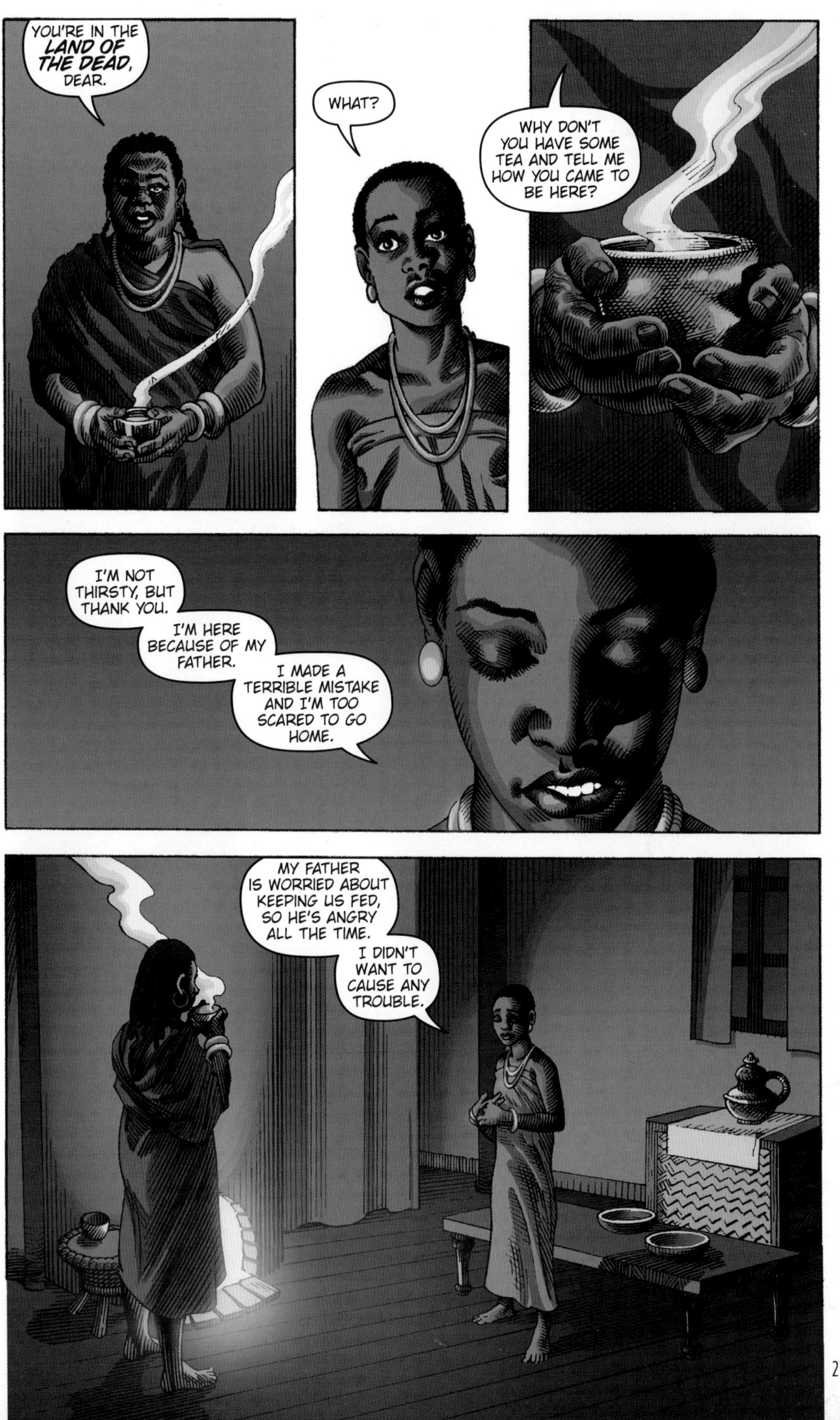
YOU'RE IN THE LAND OF THE DEAD, DEAR.
WHAT?
WHY DON'T YOU HAVE SOME TEA AND TELL ME HOW YOU CAME TO BE HERE?
I'M NOT THIRSTY, BUT THANK YOU.
I'M HERE BECAUSE OF MY FATHER.
I MADE A TERRIBLE MISTAKE AND I'M TOO SCARED TO GO HOME.
MY FATHER IS WORRIED ABOUT KEEPING US FED, SO HE'S ANGRY ALL THE TIME.
I DIDN'T WANT TO CAUSE ANY TROUBLE.

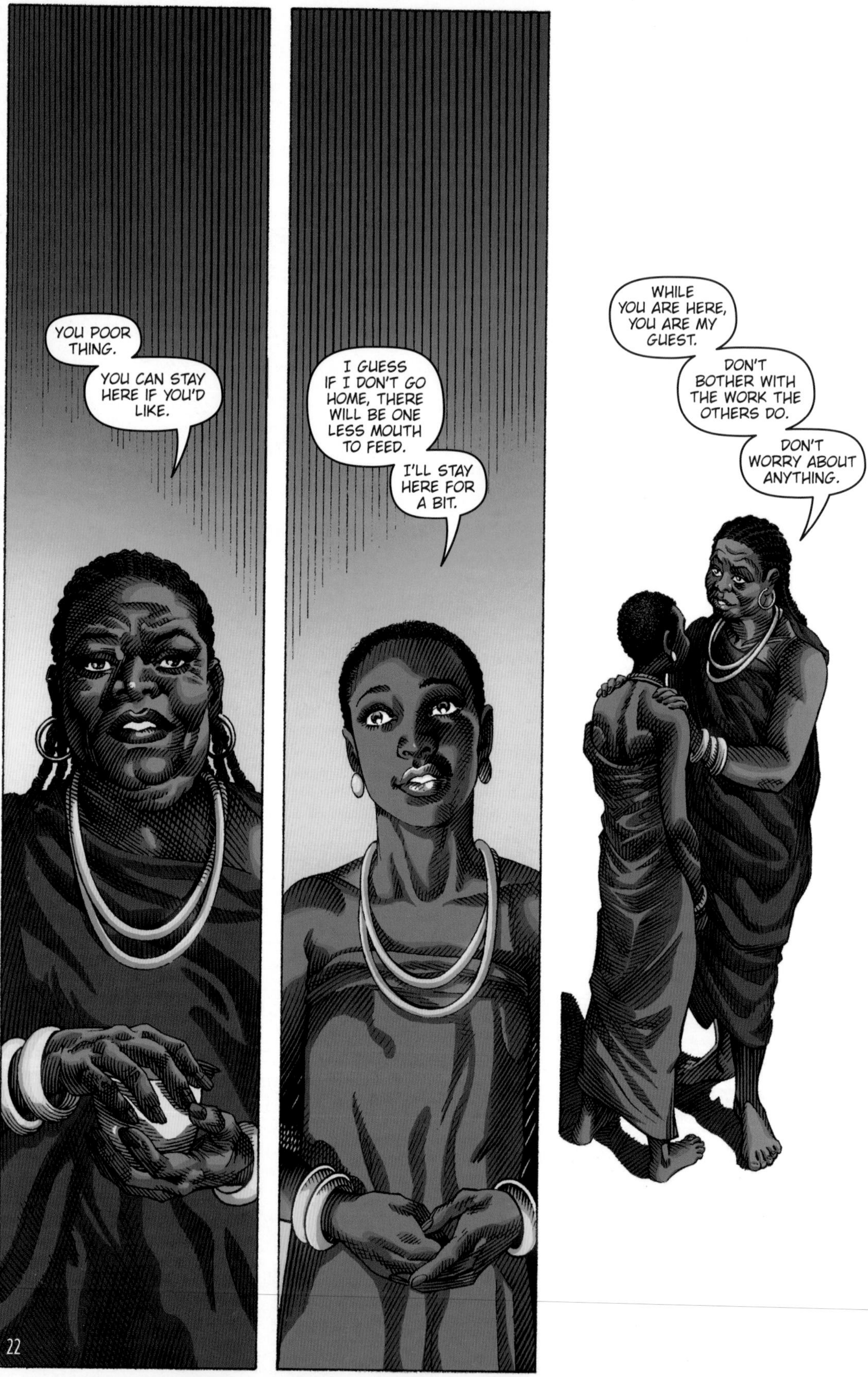
YOU POOR THING.
YOU CAN STAY HERE IF YOU'D LIKE.
I GUESS IF I DON'T GO HOME, THERE WILL BE ONE LESS MOUTH TO FEED.
I'LL STAY HERE FOR A BIT.
WHILE YOU ARE HERE, YOU ARE MY GUEST.
DON'T BOTHER WITH THE WORK THE OTHERS DO.
DON'T WORRY ABOUT ANYTHING.

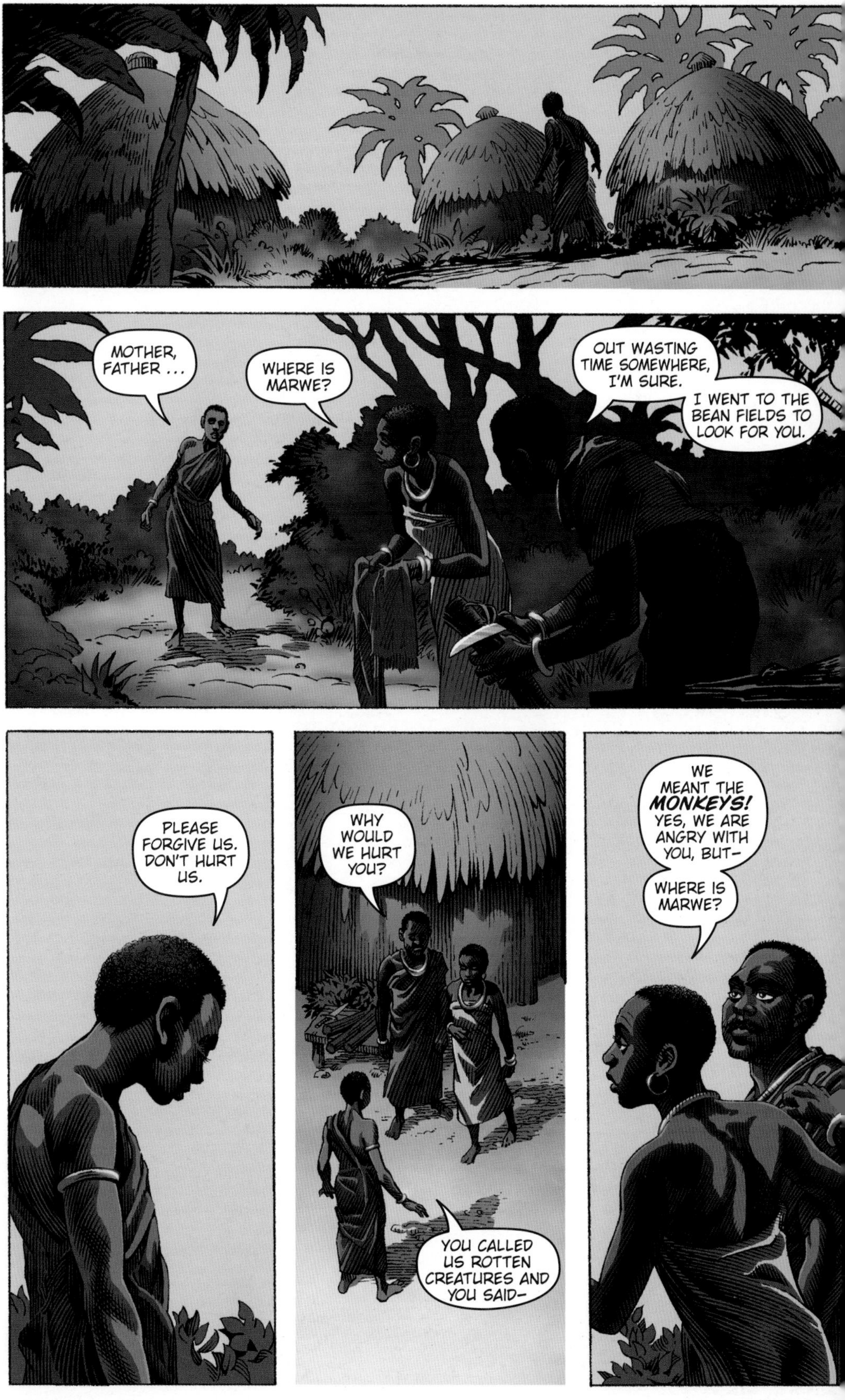
MOTHER, FATHER . . .
WHERE IS MARWE?
OUT WASTING TIME SOMEWHERE, I'M SURE.
I WENT TO THE BEAN FIELDS TO LOOK FOR YOU.
PLEASE FORGIVE US. DON'T HURT US.
WHY WOULD WE HURT YOU?
YOU CALLED US ROTTEN CREATURES AND YOU SAID–
WE MEANT THE MONKEYS! YES, WE ARE ANGRY WITH YOU, BUT–
WHERE IS MARWE?

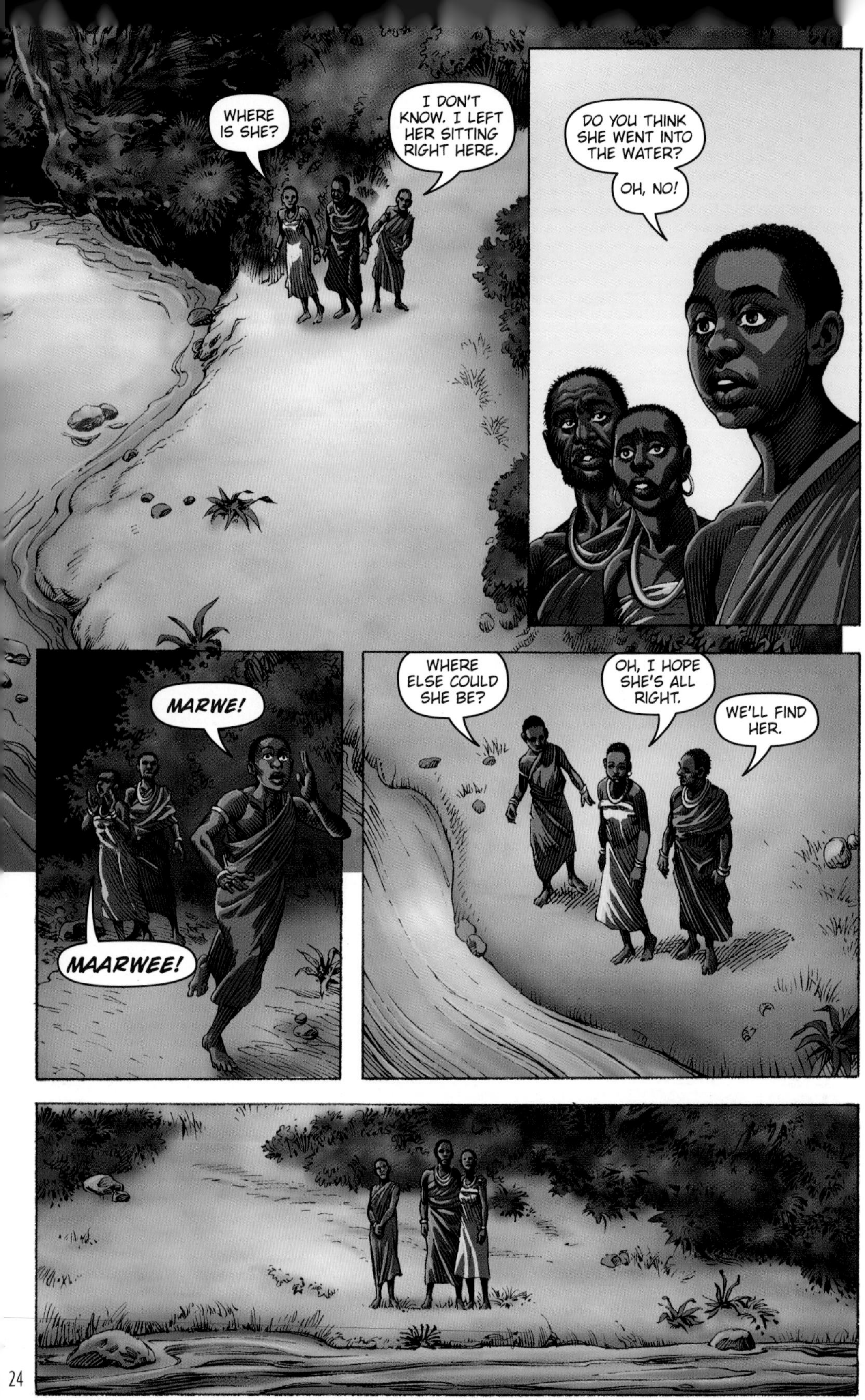
WHERE IS SHE?
I DON'T KNOW. I LEFT HER SITTING RIGHT HERE.
DO YOU THINK SHE WENT INTO THE WATER?
OH, NO!
MARWE!
MAARWEE!
WHERE ELSE COULD SHE BE?
OH, I HOPE SHE'S ALL RIGHT.
WE'LL FIND HER.

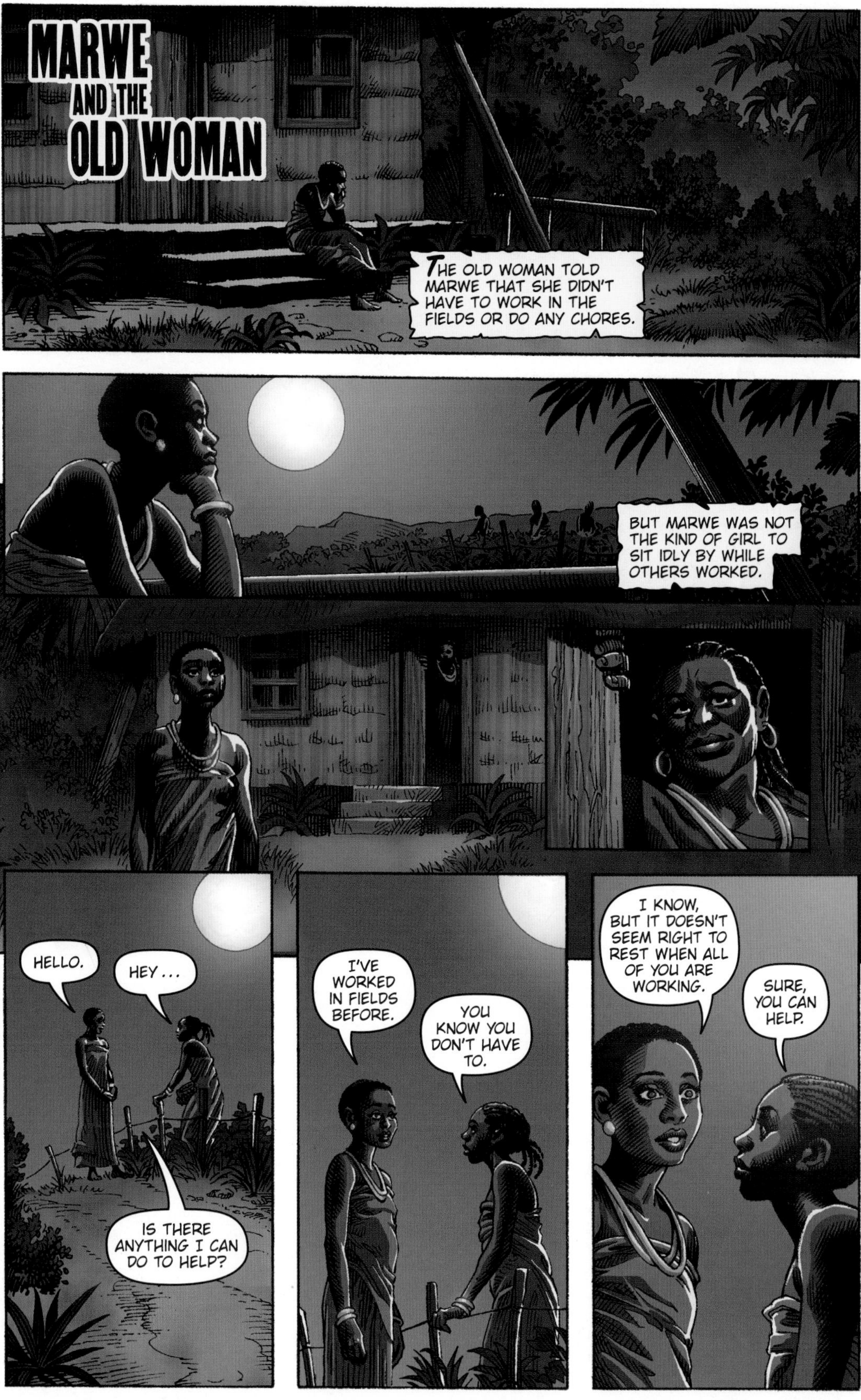
MARWE AND THE OLD WOMAN
THE OLD WOMAN TOLD MARWE THAT SHE DIDN'T HAVE TO WORK IN THE FIELDS OR DO ANY CHORES.
BUT MARWE WAS NOT THE KIND OF GIRL TO SIT IDLY BY WHILE OTHERS WORKED.
HELLO.
HEY ...
IS THERE ANYTHING I CAN DO TO HELP?
I'VE WORKED IN FIELDS BEFORE.
YOU KNOW YOU DON'T HAVE TO.
I KNOW, BUT IT DOESN'T SEEM RIGHT TO REST WHEN ALL OF YOU ARE WORKING.
SURE, YOU CAN HELP.

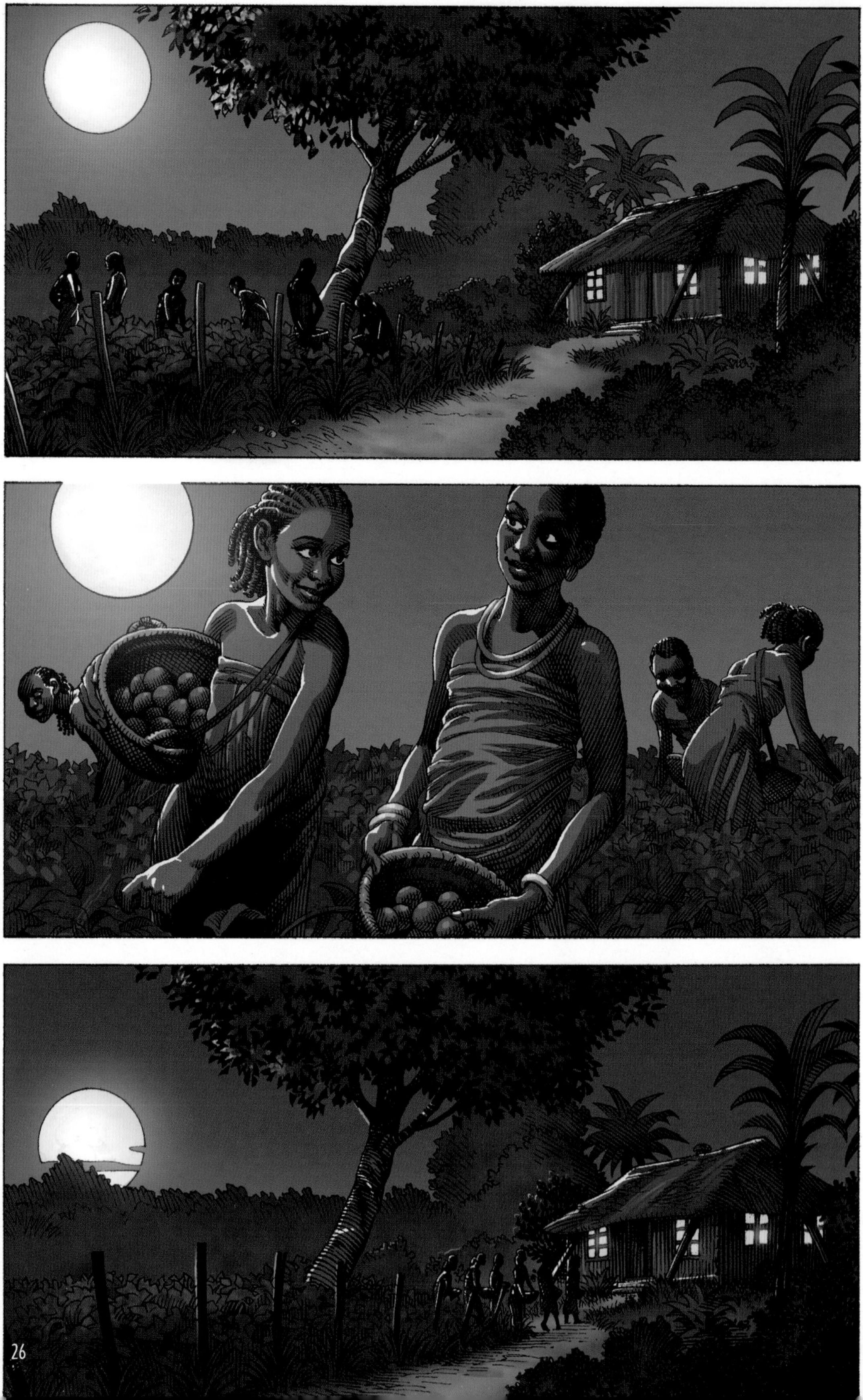

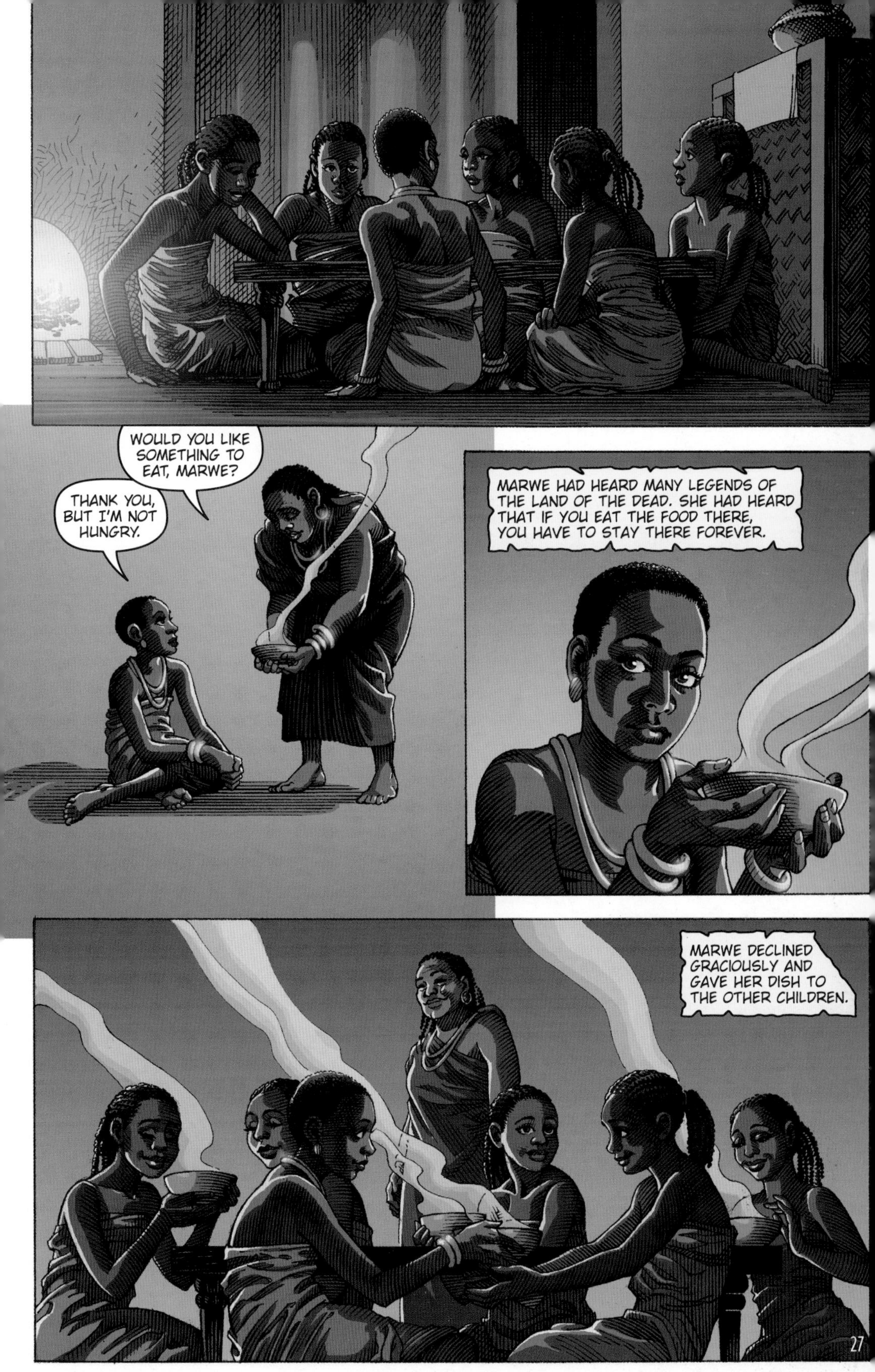
WOULD YOU LIKE SOMETHING TO EAT, MARWE?
THANK YOU, BUT I'M NOT HUNGRY.
MARWE HAD HEARD MANY LEGENDS OF THE LAND OF THE DEAD. SHE HAD HEARD THAT IF YOU EAT THE FOOD THERE, YOU HAVE TO STAY THERE FOREVER.
MARWE DECLINED GRACIOUSLY AND GAVE HER DISH TO THE OTHER CHILDREN.

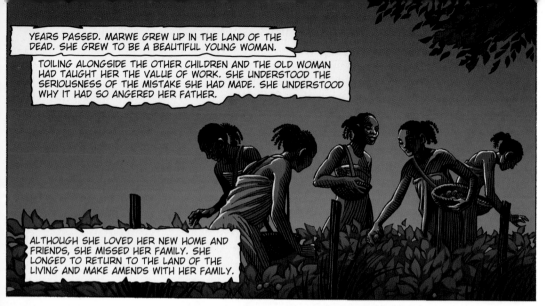

YEARS PASSED. MARWE GREW UP IN THE LAND OF THE DEAD. SHE GREW TO BE A BEAUTIFUL YOUNG WOMAN.

TOILING ALONGSIDE THE OTHER CHILDREN AND THE OLD WOMAN HAD TAUGHT HER THE VALUE OF WORK. SHE UNDERSTOOD THE SERIOUSNESS OF THE MISTAKE SHE HAD MADE. SHE UNDERSTOOD WHY IT HAD SO ANGERED HER FATHER.

ALTHOUGH SHE LOVED HER NEW HOME AND FRIENDS, SHE MISSED HER FAMILY. SHE LONGED TO RETURN TO THE LAND OF THE LIVING AND MAKE AMENDS WITH HER FAMILY.

COME ON, IT'S TIME TO GO HOME.

I THINK YOU MIGHT BE RIGHT.

WHAT DO YOU MEAN?

I THINK IT'S TIME FOR ME TO GO BACK TO MY *HOME*.

IN THE *REAL WORLD*.

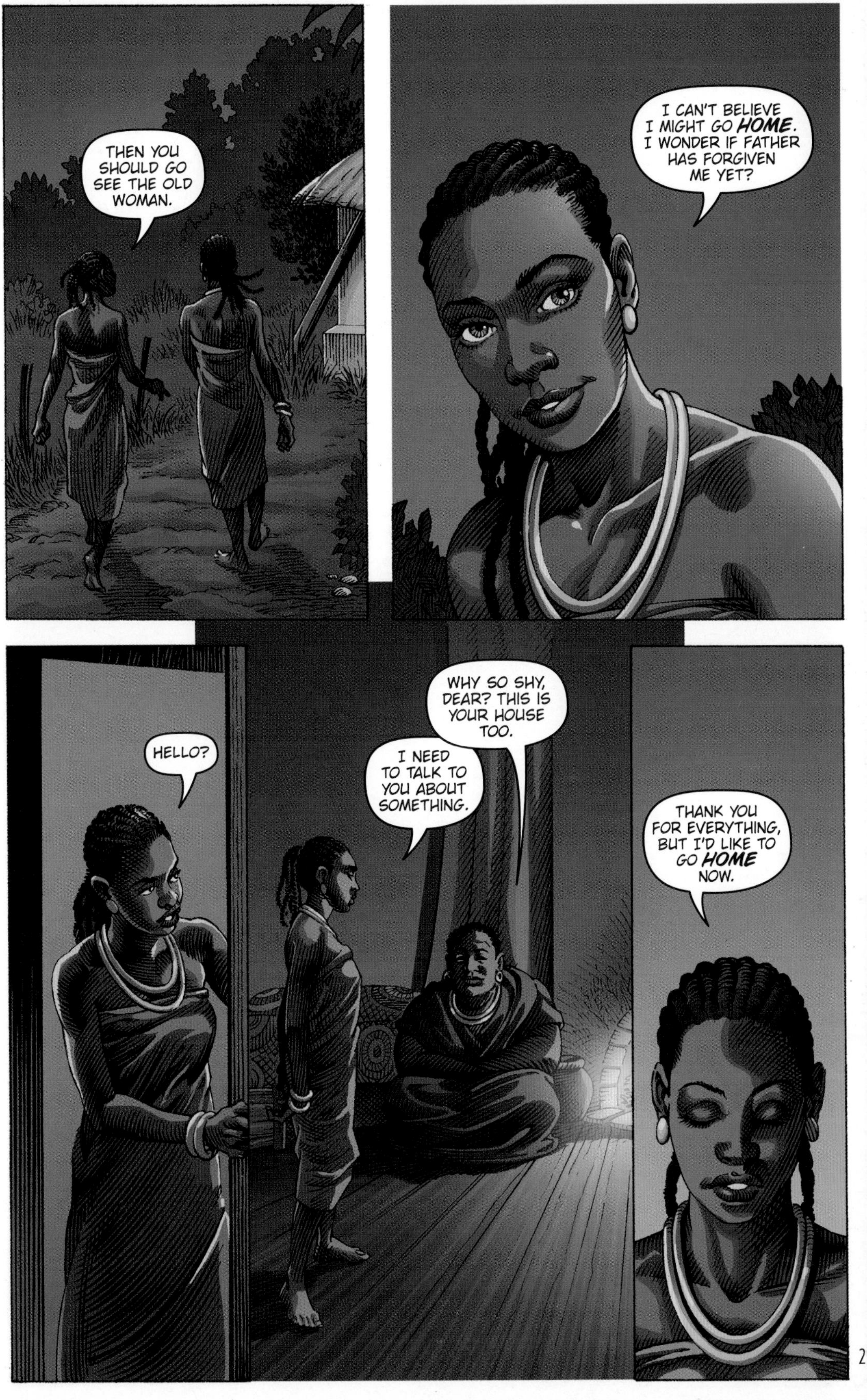
THEN YOU SHOULD GO SEE THE OLD WOMAN.
I CAN'T BELIEVE I MIGHT GO HOME. I WONDER IF FATHER HAS FORGIVEN ME YET?
HELLO?
WHY SO SHY, DEAR? THIS IS YOUR HOUSE TOO.
I NEED TO TALK TO YOU ABOUT SOMETHING.
THANK YOU FOR EVERYTHING, BUT I'D LIKE TO GO HOME NOW.

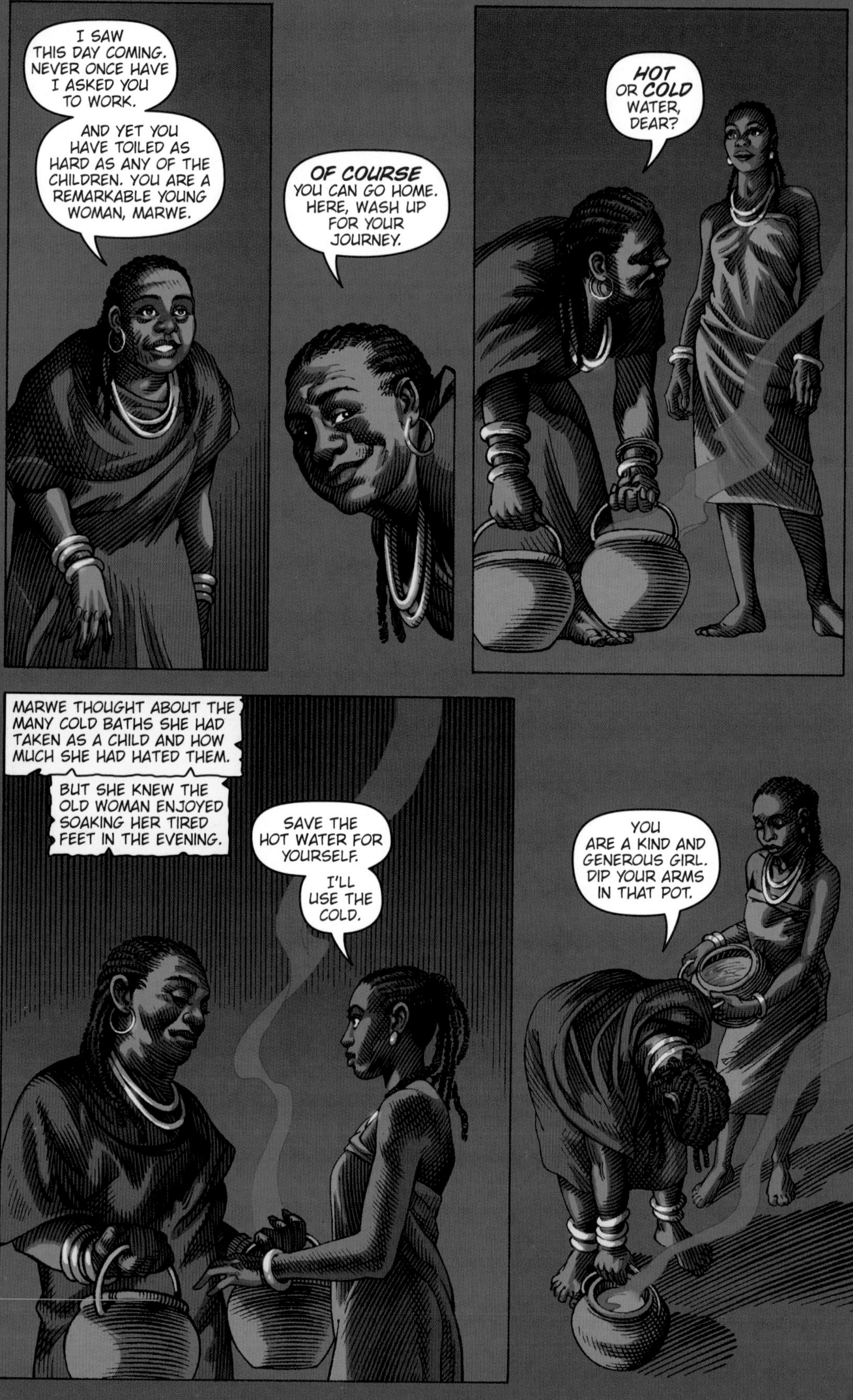
I SAW THIS DAY COMING. NEVER ONCE HAVE I ASKED YOU TO WORK.
AND YET YOU HAVE TOILED AS HARD AS ANY OF THE CHILDREN. YOU ARE A REMARKABLE YOUNG WOMAN, MARWE.
OF COURSE YOU CAN GO HOME. HERE, WASH UP FOR YOUR JOURNEY.
HOT OR COLD WATER, DEAR?
MARWE THOUGHT ABOUT THE MANY COLD BATHS SHE HAD TAKEN AS A CHILD AND HOW MUCH SHE HAD HATED THEM.
BUT SHE KNEW THE OLD WOMAN ENJOYED SOAKING HER TIRED FEET IN THE EVENING.
SAVE THE HOT WATER FOR YOURSELF.
I'LL USE THE COLD.
YOU ARE A KIND AND GENEROUS GIRL. DIP YOUR ARMS IN THAT POT.

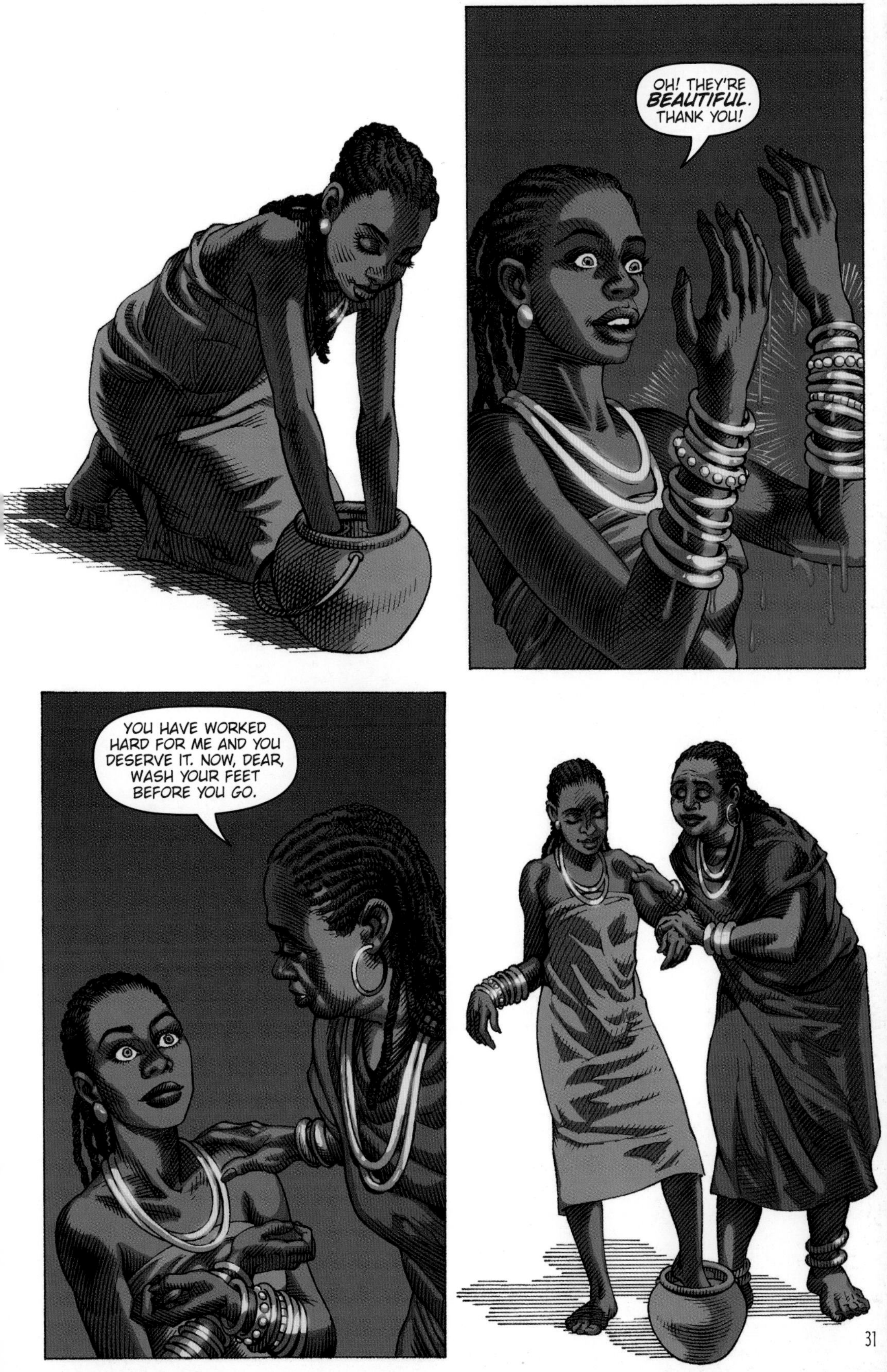
OH! THEY'RE BEAUTIFUL. THANK YOU!
YOU HAVE WORKED HARD FOR ME AND YOU DESERVE IT. NOW, DEAR, WASH YOUR FEET BEFORE YOU GO.

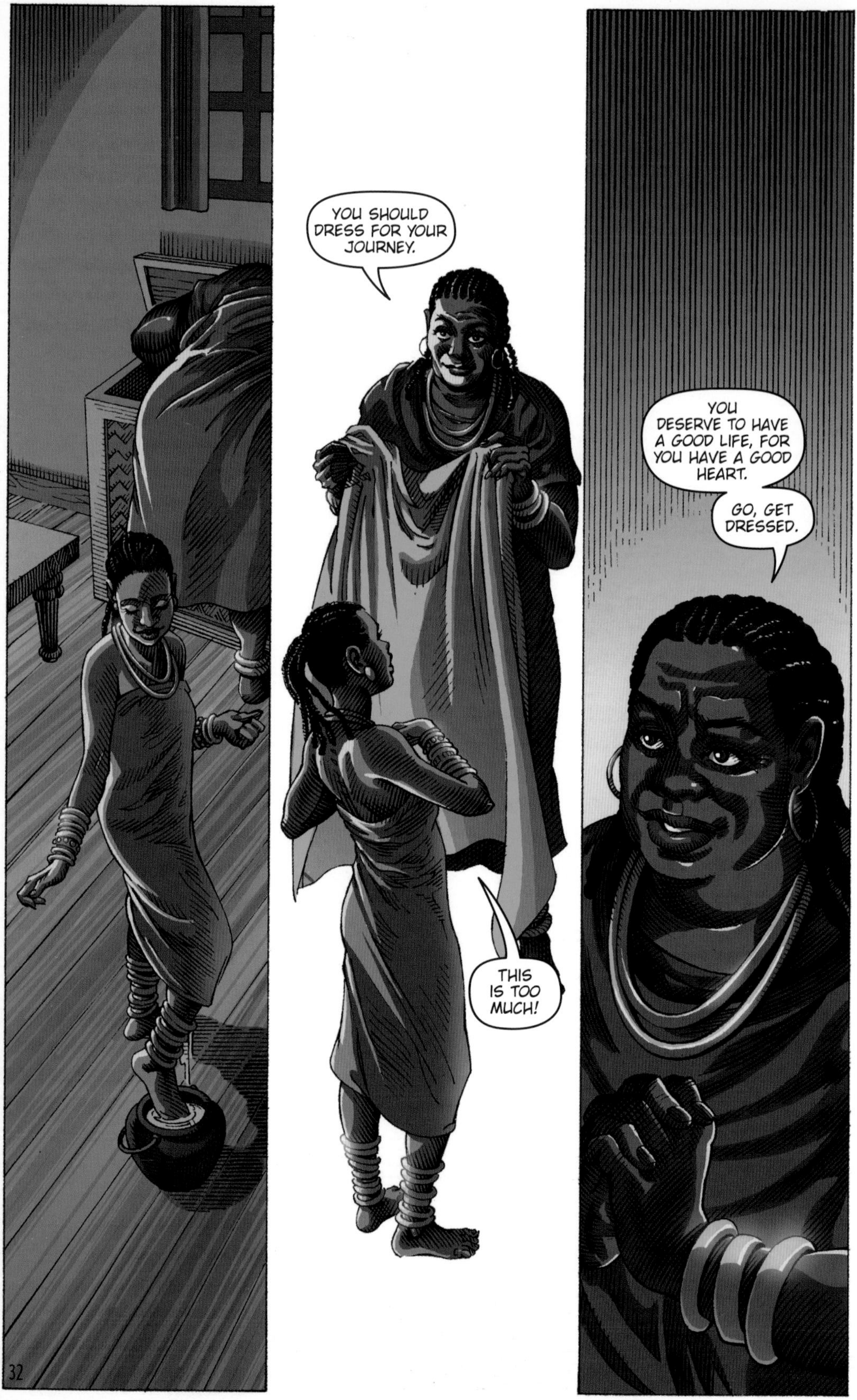
YOU SHOULD DRESS FOR YOUR JOURNEY.
THIS IS TOO MUCH!
YOU DESERVE TO HAVE A GOOD LIFE, FOR YOU HAVE A GOOD HEART.
GO, GET DRESSED.

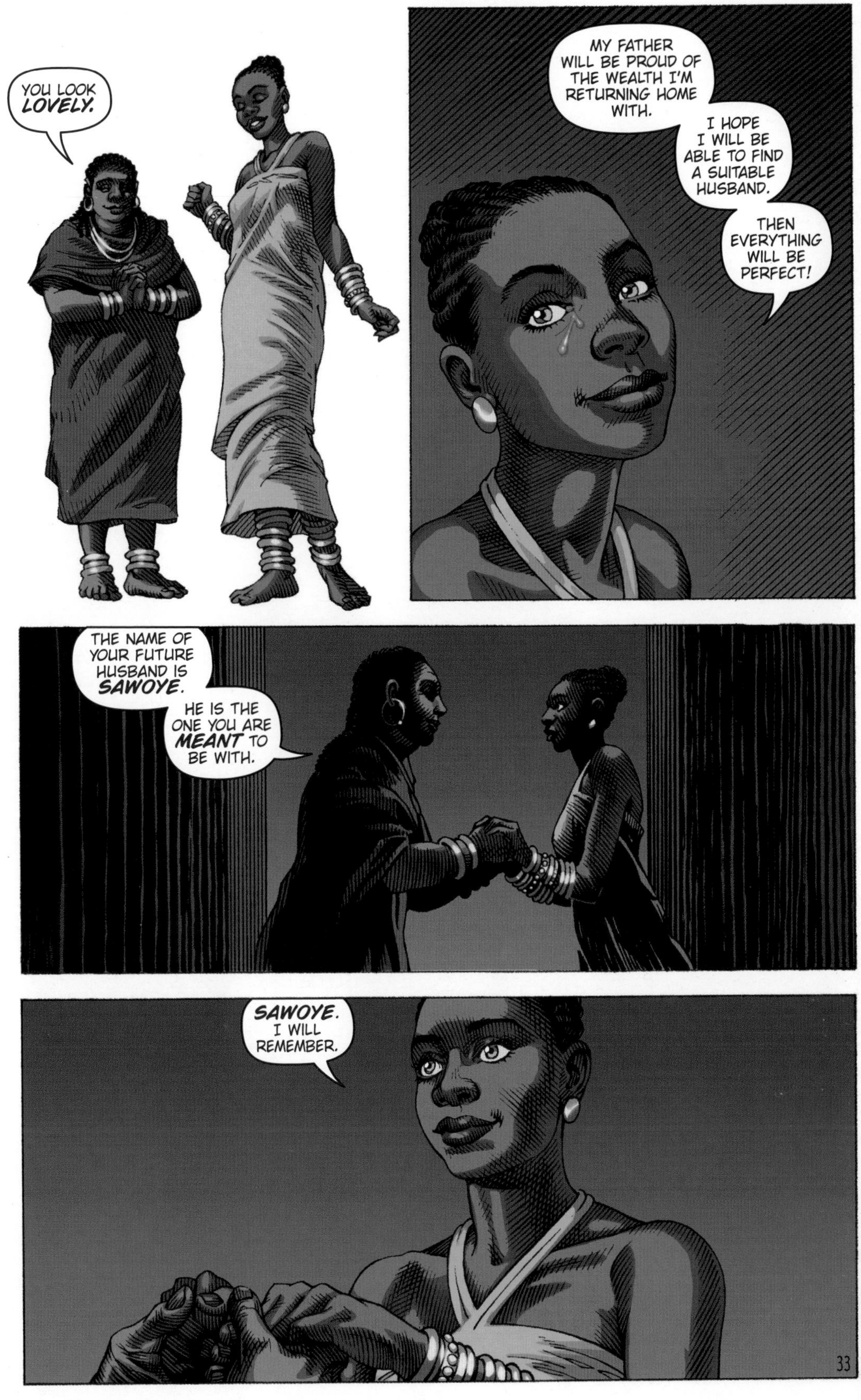

YOU LOOK LOVELY.
MY FATHER WILL BE PROUD OF THE WEALTH I'M RETURNING HOME WITH.
I HOPE I WILL BE ABLE TO FIND A SUITABLE HUSBAND.
THEN EVERYTHING WILL BE PERFECT!
THE NAME OF YOUR FUTURE HUSBAND IS SAWOYE.
HE IS THE ONE YOU ARE MEANT TO BE WITH.
SAWOYE. I WILL REMEMBER.

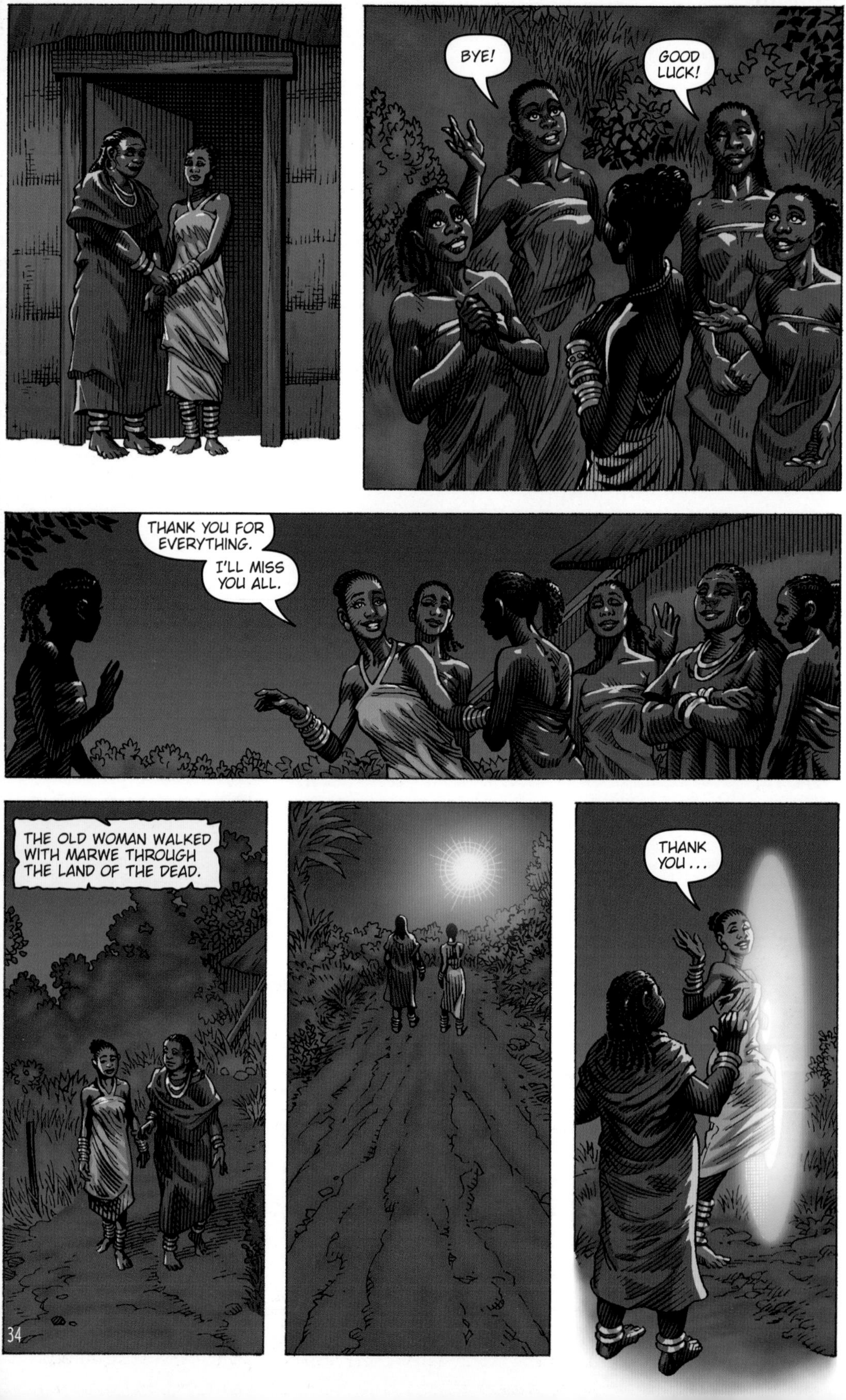
BYE!
GOOD LUCK!
THANK YOU FOR EVERYTHING.
I'LL MISS YOU ALL.
THE OLD WOMAN WALKED WITH MARWE THROUGH THE LAND OF THE DEAD.
THANK YOU . . .

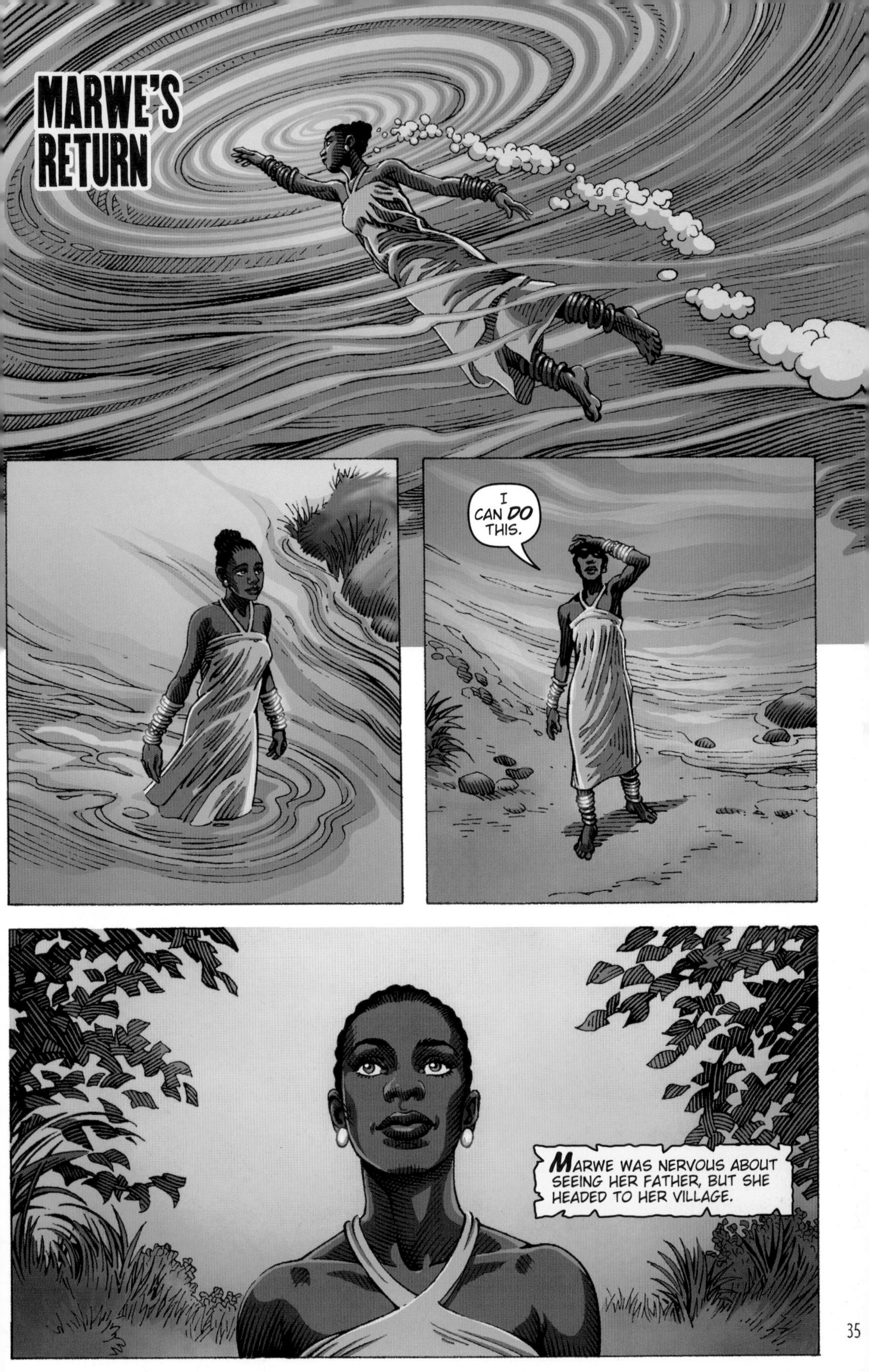
MARWE'S RETURN
I CAN DO THIS.
MARWE WAS NERVOUS ABOUT SEEING HER FATHER, BUT SHE HEADED TO HER VILLAGE.

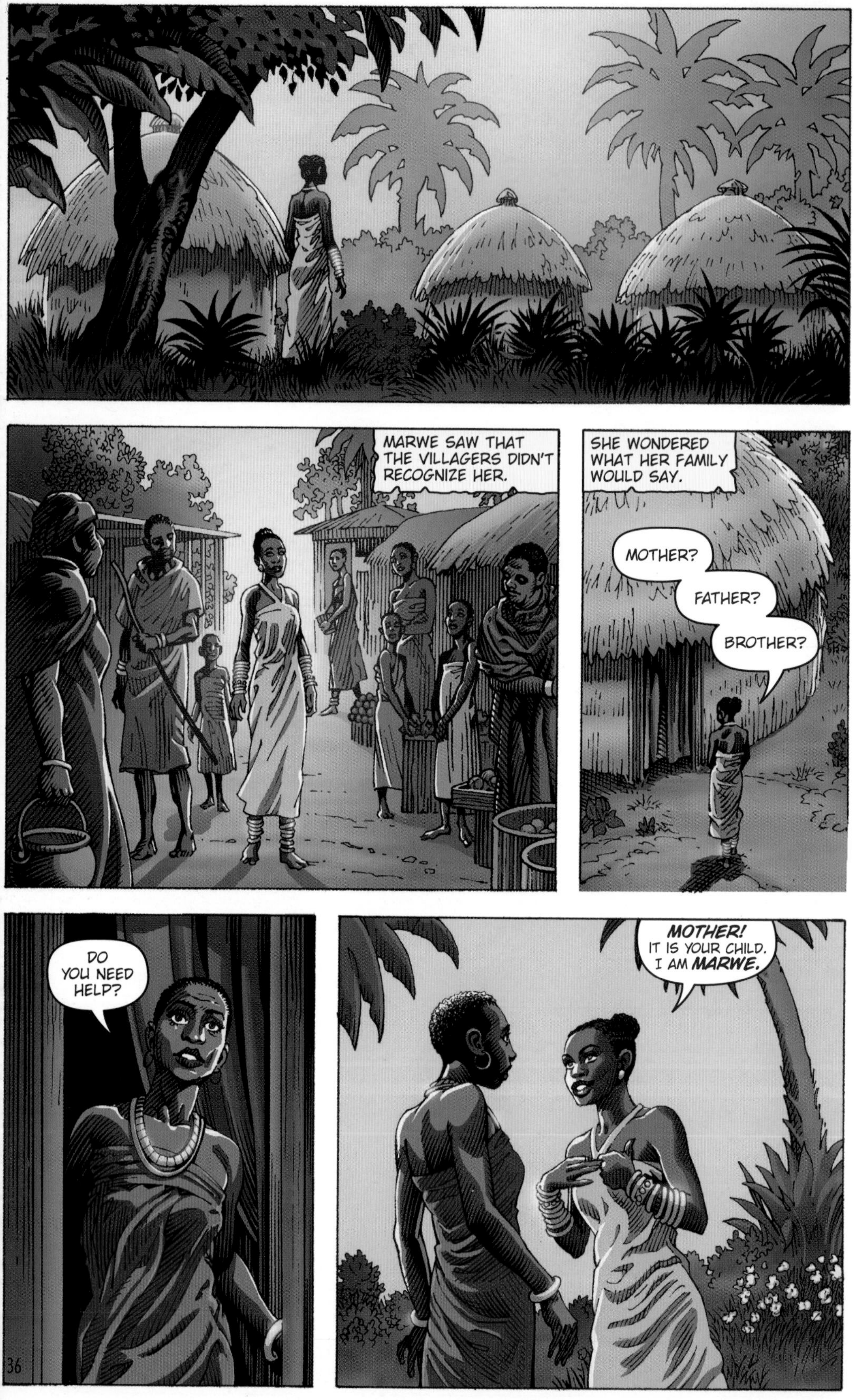
MARWE SAW THAT THE VILLAGERS DIDN'T RECOGNIZE HER.
SHE WONDERED WHAT HER FAMILY WOULD SAY.
MOTHER?
FATHER?
BROTHER?
DO YOU NEED HELP?
MOTHER! IT IS YOUR CHILD. I AM MARWE.

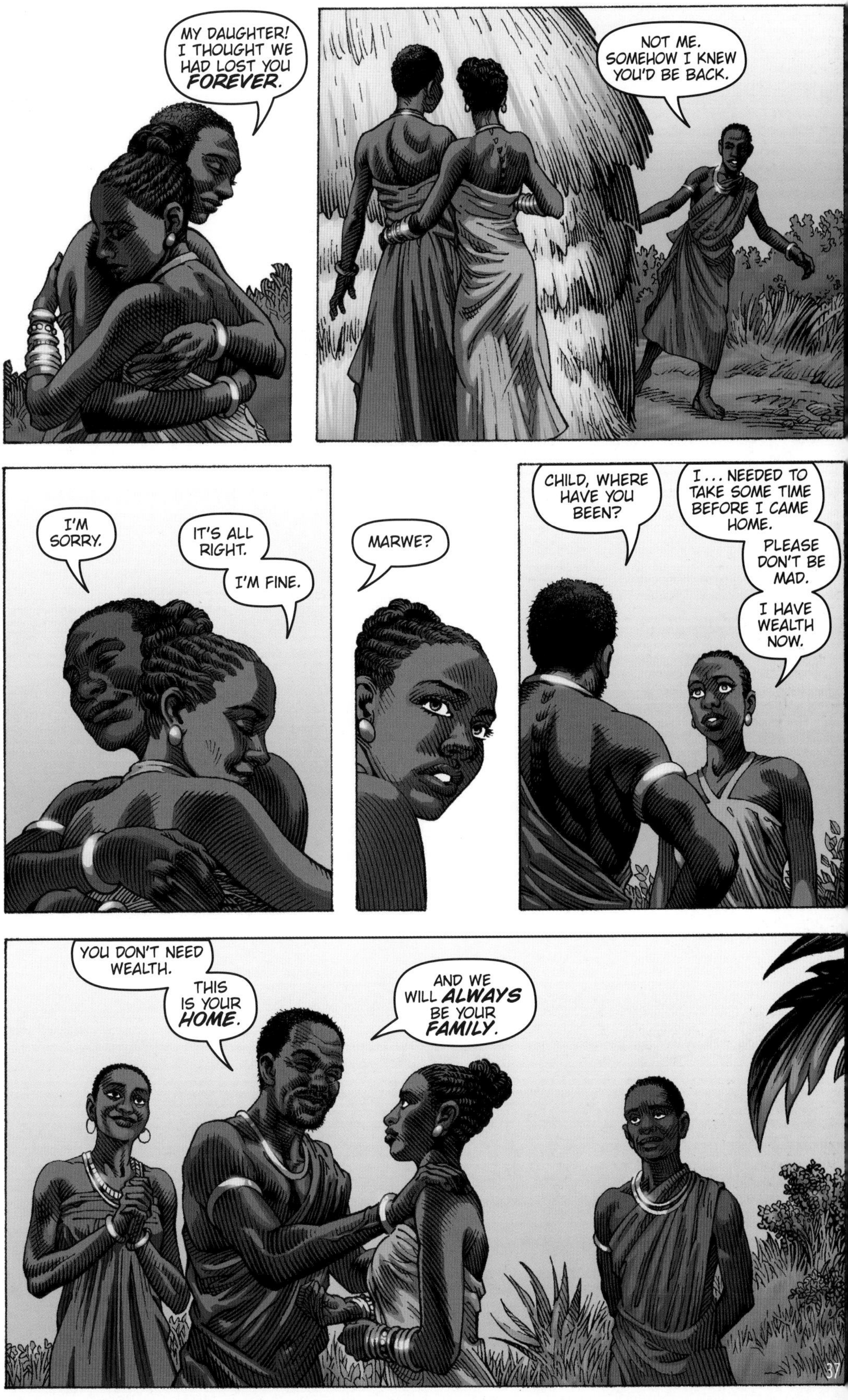
MY DAUGHTER! I THOUGHT WE HAD LOST YOU FOREVER.
NOT ME. SOMEHOW I KNEW YOU'D BE BACK.
I'M SORRY.
IT'S ALL RIGHT.
I'M FINE.
MARWE?
CHILD, WHERE HAVE YOU BEEN?
I . . . NEEDED TO TAKE SOME TIME BEFORE I CAME HOME.
PLEASE DON'T BE MAD.
I HAVE WEALTH NOW.
YOU DON'T NEED WEALTH.
THIS IS YOUR HOME.
AND WE WILL ALWAYS BE YOUR FAMILY.

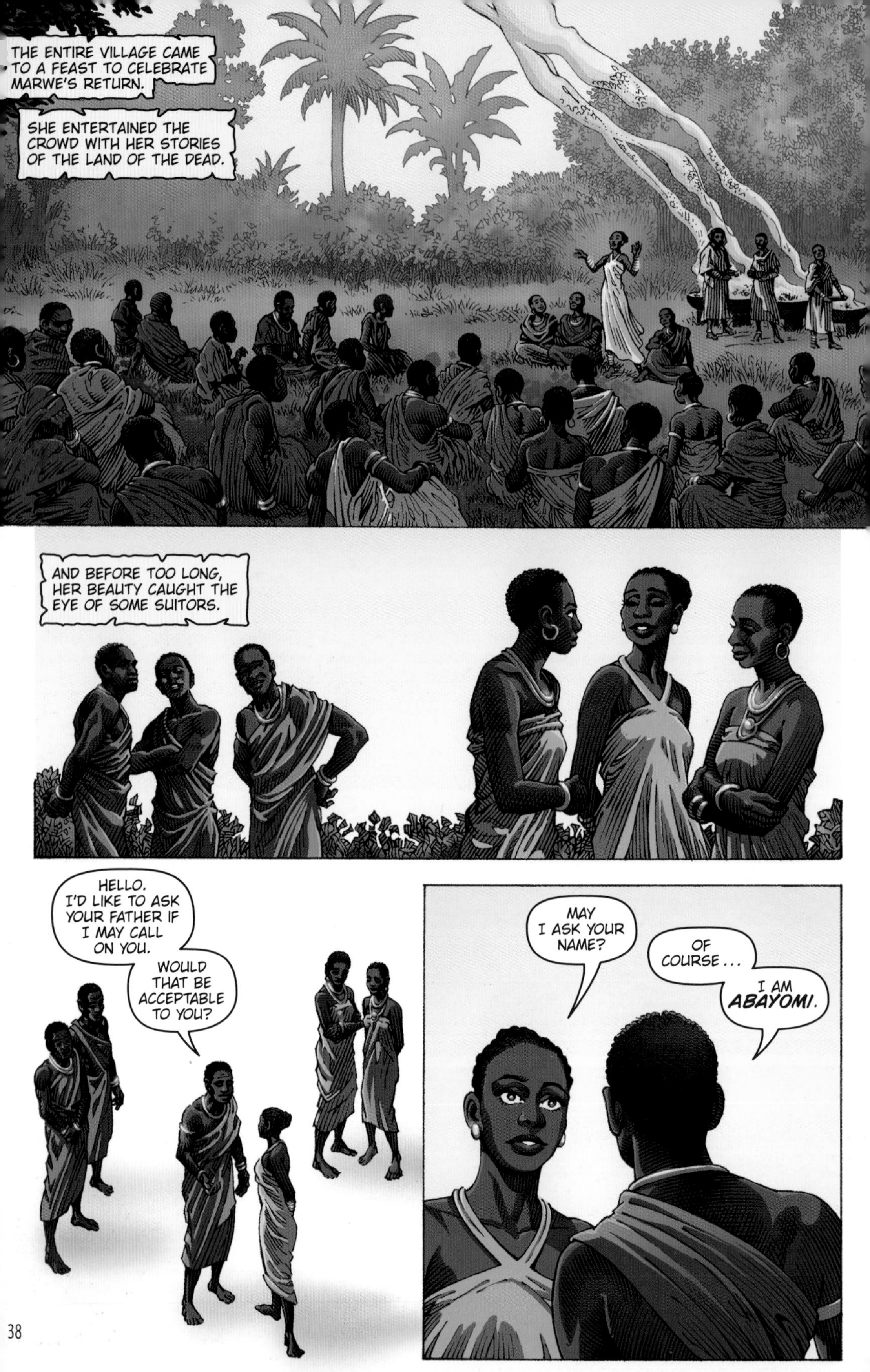
THE ENTIRE VILLAGE CAME TO A FEAST TO CELEBRATE MARWE'S RETURN.
SHE ENTERTAINED THE CROWD WITH HER STORIES OF THE LAND OF THE DEAD.
AND BEFORE TOO LONG, HER BEAUTY CAUGHT THE EYE OF SOME SUITORS.
HELLO. I'D LIKE TO ASK YOUR FATHER IF I MAY CALL ON YOU.
WOULD THAT BE ACCEPTABLE TO YOU?
MAY I ASK YOUR NAME?
OF COURSE . . .
I AM ***ABAYOMI***.

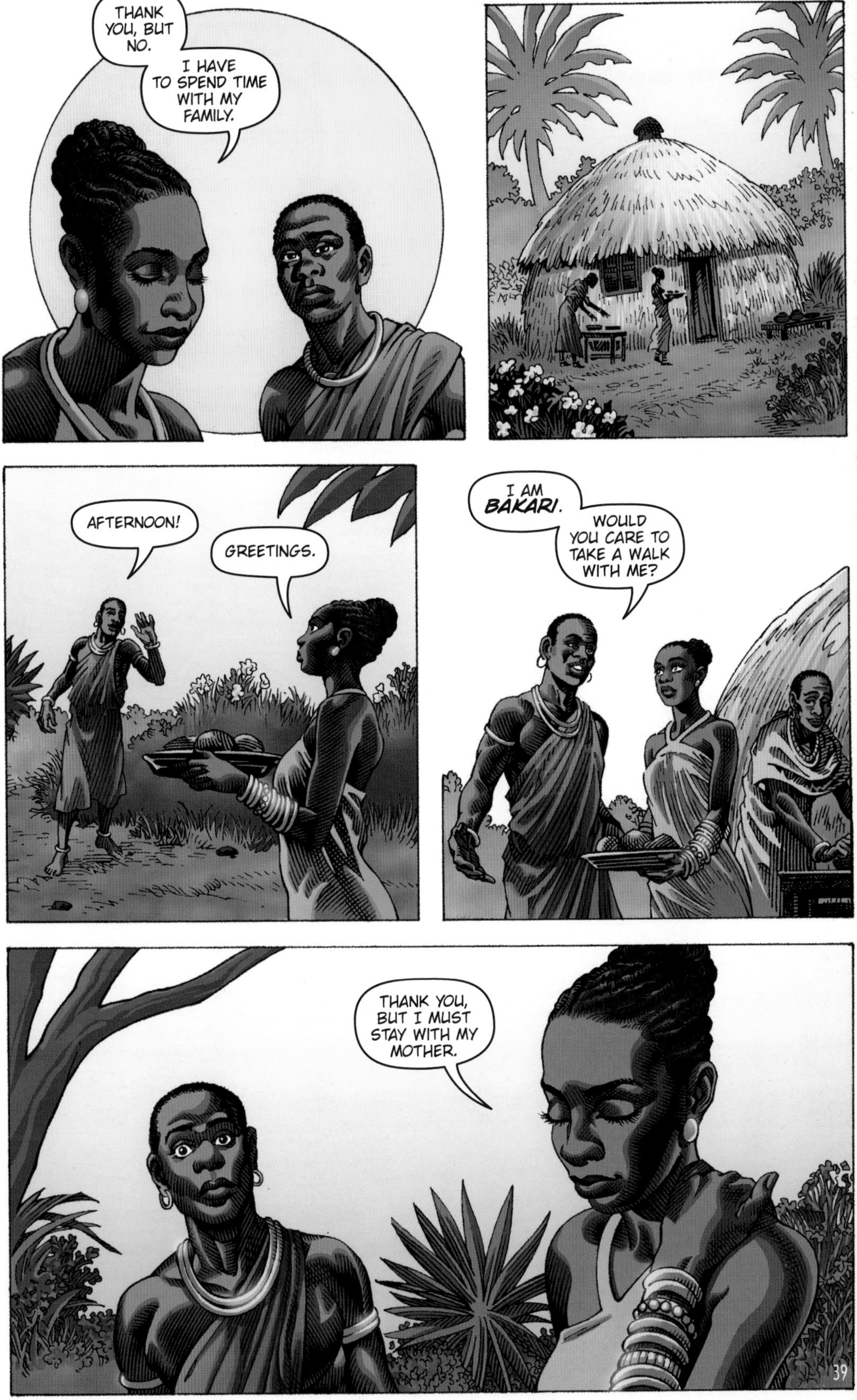
THANK YOU, BUT NO.
I HAVE TO SPEND TIME WITH MY FAMILY.
AFTERNOON!
GREETINGS.
I AM BAKARI.
WOULD YOU CARE TO TAKE A WALK WITH ME?
THANK YOU, BUT I MUST STAY WITH MY MOTHER.

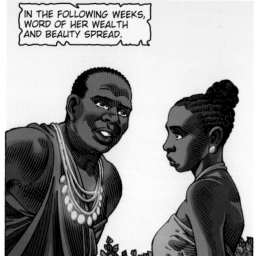

IN THE FOLLOWING WEEKS, WORD OF HER WEALTH AND BEAUTY SPREAD.

AND MANY SUITORS APPROACHED MARWE.

BUT NONE OF THEM WAS SAWOYE.

AND SHE TURNED THEM ALL AWAY.

MARWE AND SAWOYE

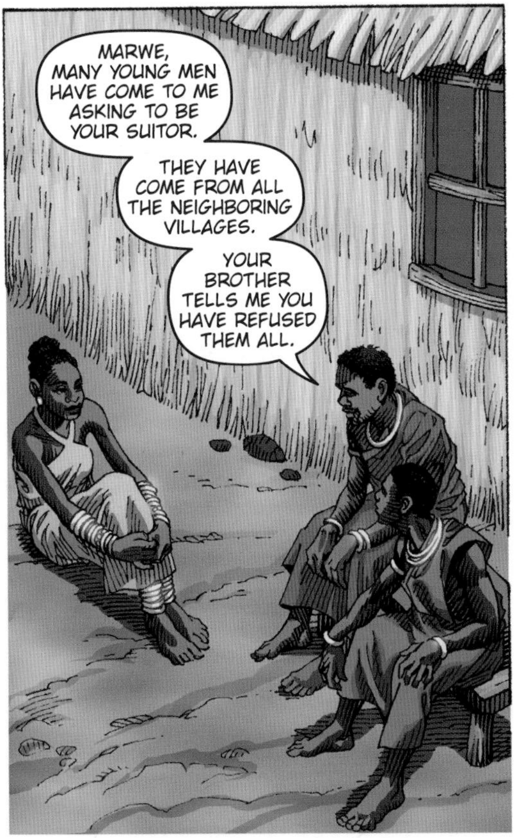
MARWE, MANY YOUNG MEN HAVE COME TO ME ASKING TO BE YOUR SUITOR.
THEY HAVE COME FROM ALL THE NEIGHBORING VILLAGES.
YOUR BROTHER TELLS ME YOU HAVE REFUSED THEM ALL.

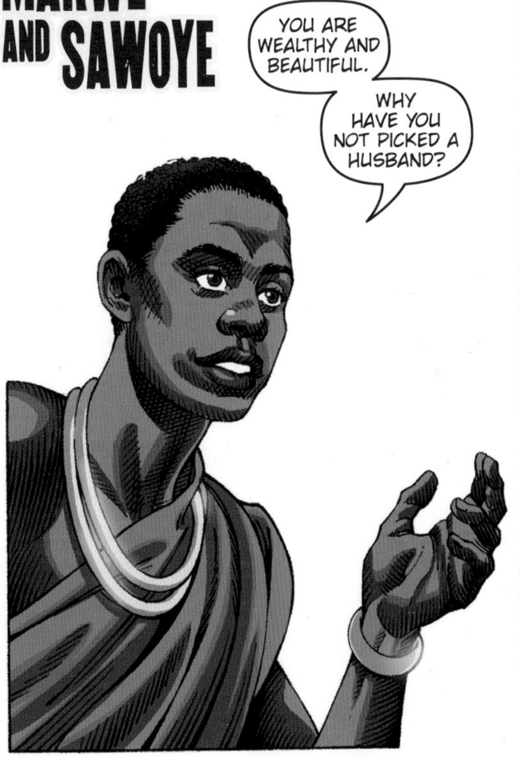
YOU ARE WEALTHY AND BEAUTIFUL.
WHY HAVE YOU NOT PICKED A HUSBAND?

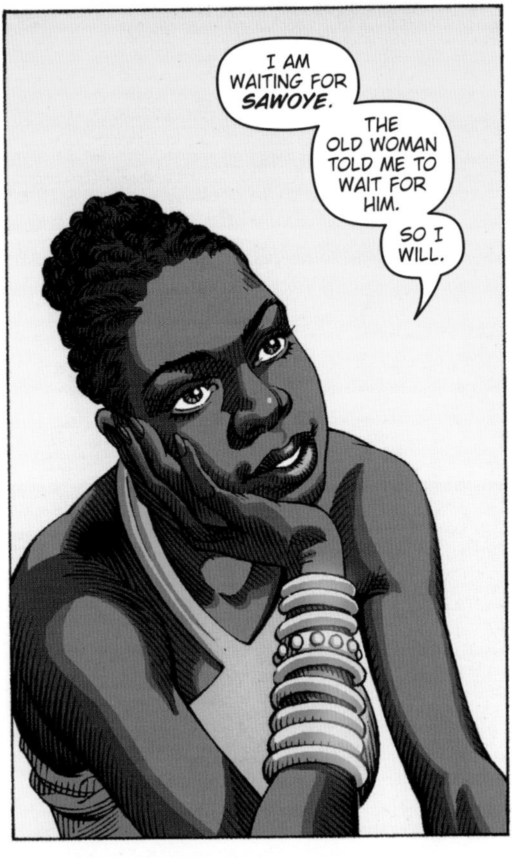
I AM WAITING FOR ***SAWOYE.***
THE OLD WOMAN TOLD ME TO WAIT FOR HIM.
SO I WILL.

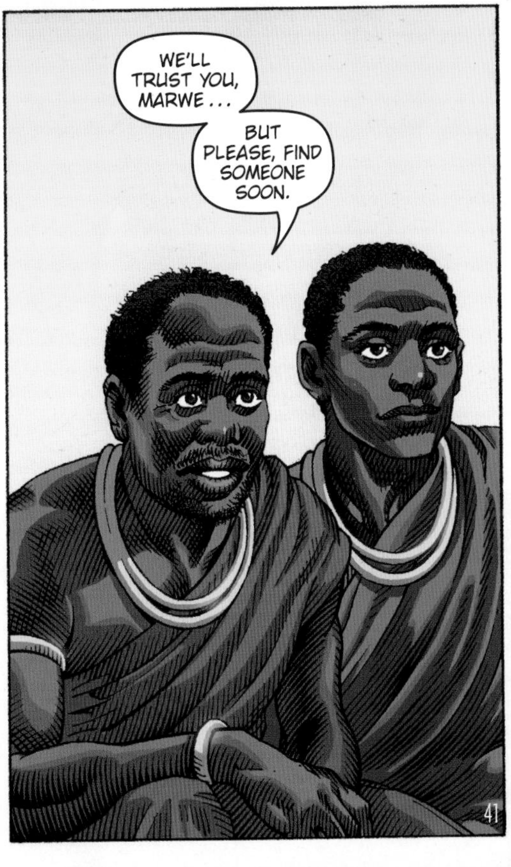
WE'LL TRUST YOU, MARWE . . .
BUT PLEASE, FIND SOMEONE SOON.

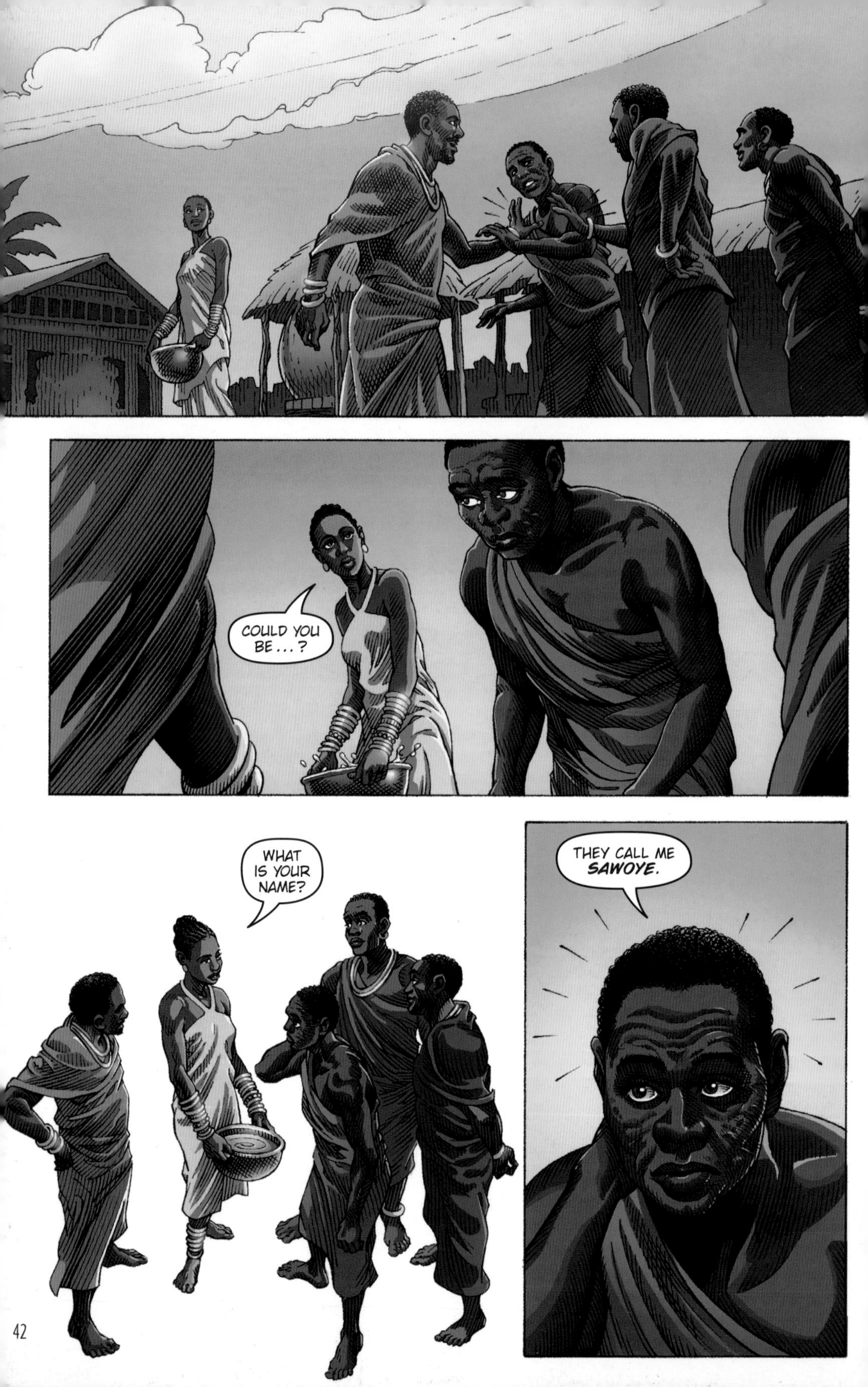
COULD YOU BE...?
WHAT IS YOUR NAME?
THEY CALL ME **SAWOYE**.

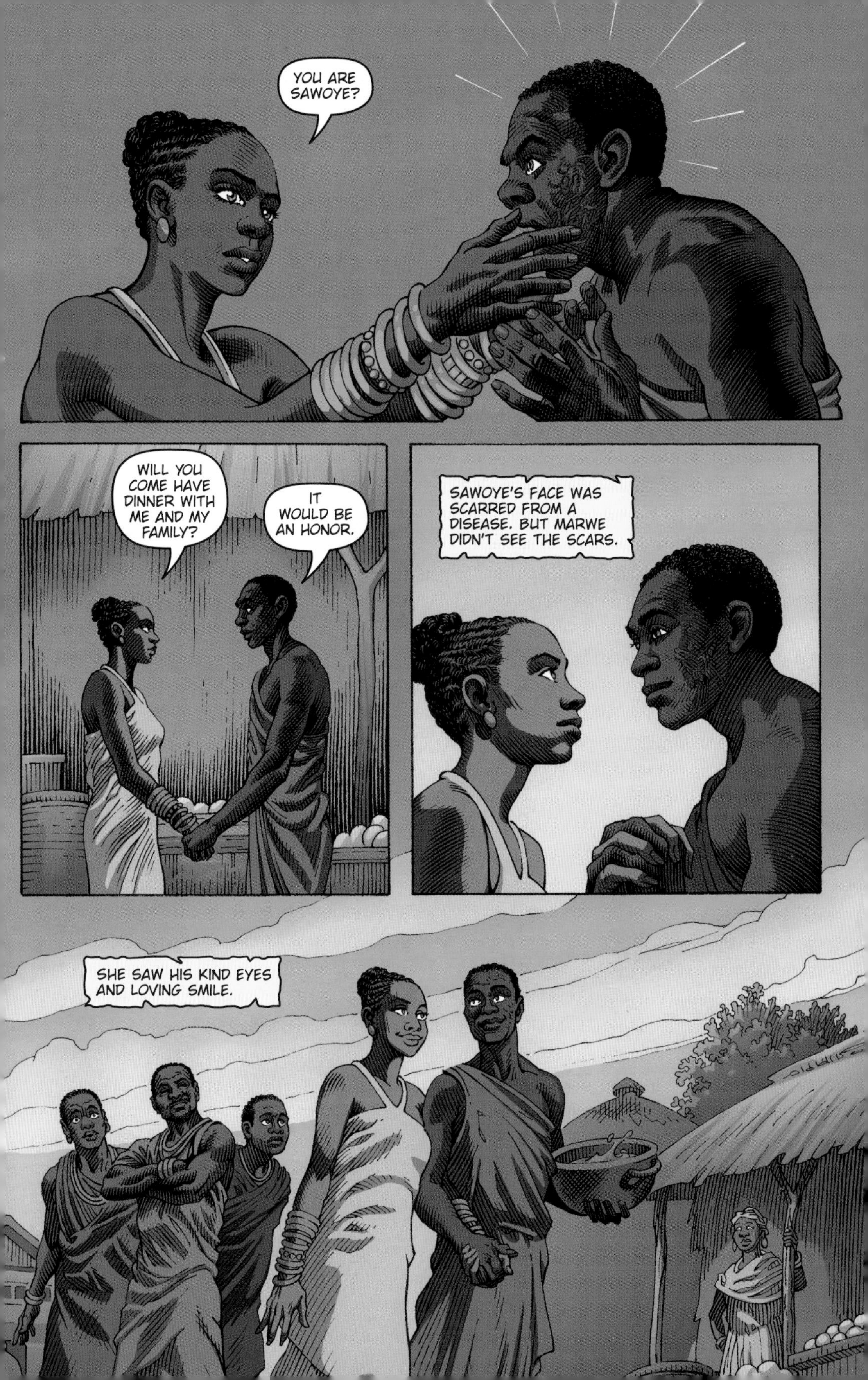
YOU ARE SAWOYE?
WILL YOU COME HAVE DINNER WITH ME AND MY FAMILY?
IT WOULD BE AN HONOR.
SAWOYE'S FACE WAS SCARRED FROM A DISEASE. BUT MARWE DIDN'T SEE THE SCARS.
SHE SAW HIS KIND EYES AND LOVING SMILE.

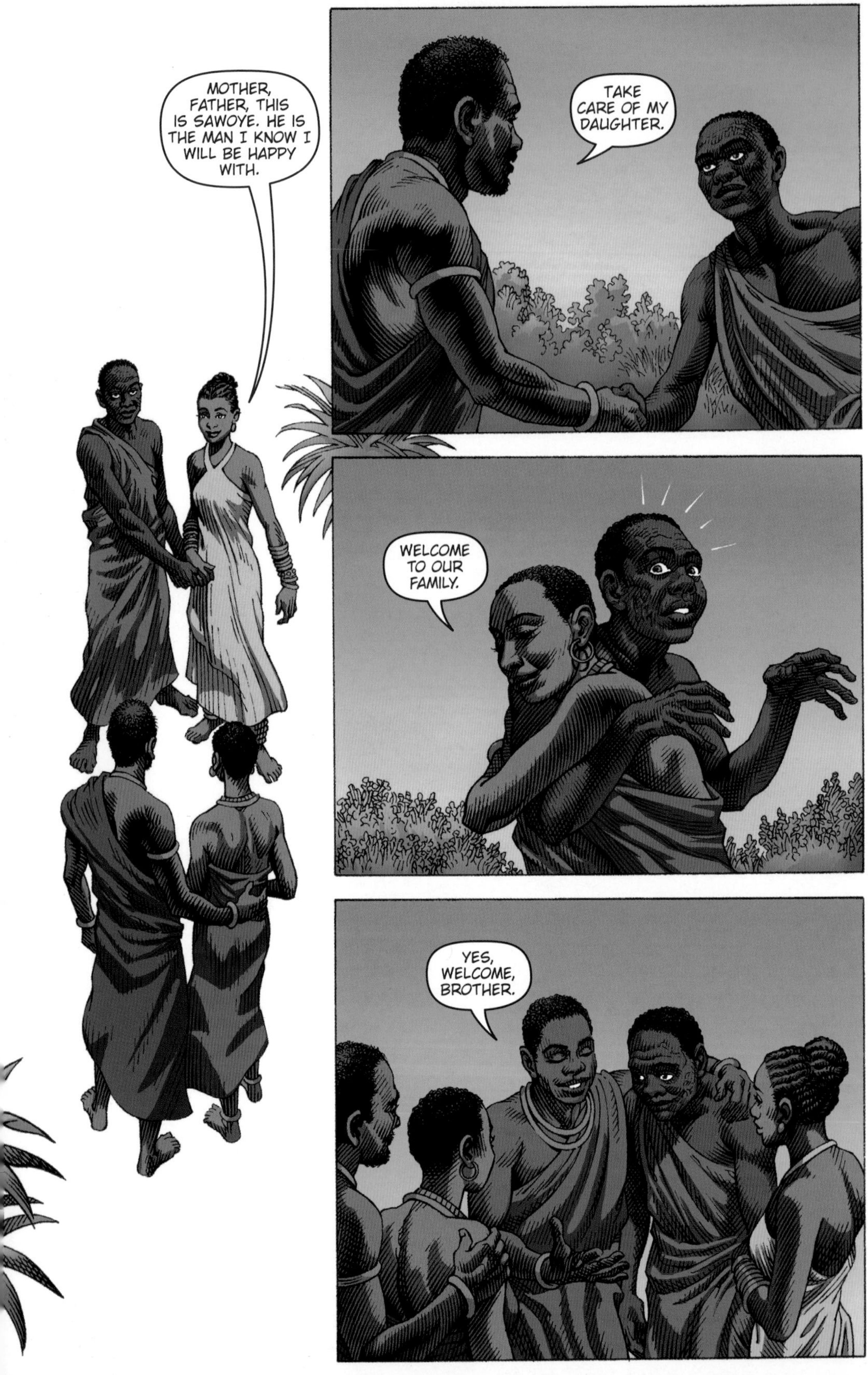
MOTHER, FATHER, THIS IS SAWOYE. HE IS THE MAN I KNOW I WILL BE HAPPY WITH.
TAKE CARE OF MY DAUGHTER.
WELCOME TO OUR FAMILY.
YES, WELCOME, BROTHER.

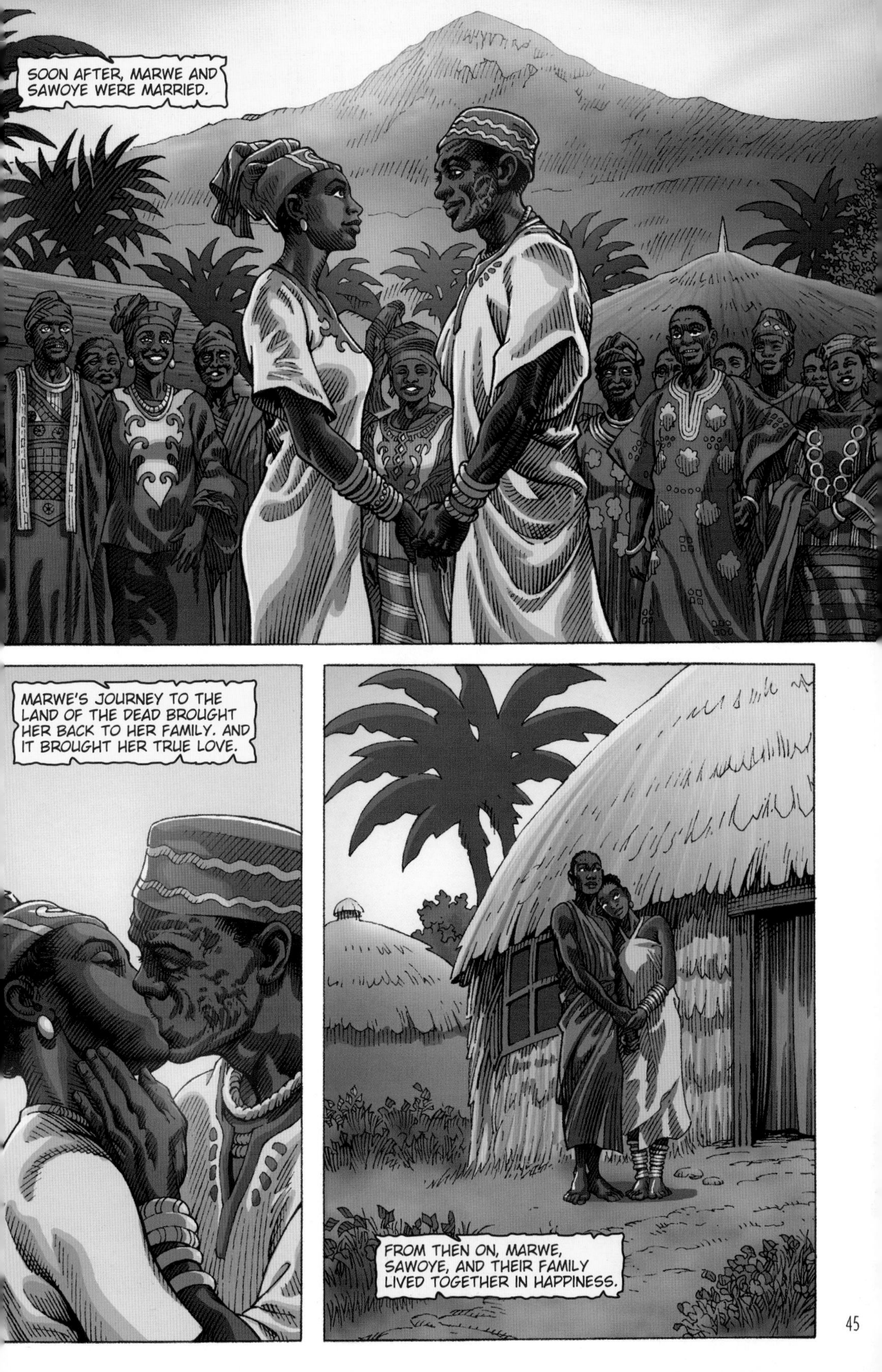
SOON AFTER, MARWE AND SAWOYE WERE MARRIED.
MARWE'S JOURNEY TO THE LAND OF THE DEAD BROUGHT HER BACK TO HER FAMILY. AND IT BROUGHT HER TRUE LOVE.
FROM THEN ON, MARWE, SAWOYE, AND THEIR FAMILY LIVED TOGETHER IN HAPPINESS.

GLOSSARY AND PRONUNCIATION GUIDE

ABAYOMI (ah-bah-*yoh*-mee): a young man in Marwe's village

BAKARI (bah-*kah*-ree): another young man in Marwe's village

BANTU (*bahn*-too): a group of languages spoken primarily in the southern half of Africa

CHAGA (*chah*-gah): a Bantu-speaking tribe in Africa. They are the third-largest ethnic group in Tanzania.

FOOTHILLS: a hilly region at the base of a mountain or mountain range

MARWE (*mar*-way): the young girl who travels to the Land of the Dead

MOUNT KILIMANJARO (*keh*-leh-mahn-*jah*-roh): the tallest mountain in Africa, in the country of Tanzania. It has two peaks, famous for being covered with snow.

MOUNT MERU (*meh*-roo): a mountain west of Mount Kilimanjaro. It is an active volcano.

RITE: a ritual, or ceremony

SAWOYE (sah-*woh*-yay): an outcast young man

SUITOR: a man who seeks to marry a specific woman; someone who courts another person.

TANZANIA (tahn-zah-*nee*-ah): a country in East Africa

CREATING *MARWE: INTO THE LAND OF THE DEAD*

Author Marie P. Croall found *Marwe: Into the Land of the Dead* to be one of her most interesting challenges to adapt, because of the shortage of written reference material and the unique storytelling style of the oral myth. She saw parallels between *Marwe* and European fairy tales such as *Sleeping Beauty* and *Snow White*, and was particularly charmed by Marwe's combination of compassion and bravery. Ray Lago's delicate pencil work was a perfect match for inker Craig Hamilton. Harold E. Scheub, professor of African Languages and Literature at the University of Wisconsin-Madison, reviewed Ray Lago's sketches for authenticity and attention to the details of Marwe's world.

FURTHER READING, WEBSITES, AND MOVIES

Grimes, Nikki. *Is It Far to Zanzibar?: Poems about Tanzania*. New York: HarperCollins, 2000. These poems about life in Tanzania—its cities, its marketplaces, its people, and their homes—are also beautifully illustrated with watercolor paintings.

Humanistic Texts: Bantu
http://www.humanistictexts.org/bantu.htm
This website shares the ideas and wisdom of people around the world and has proverbs and stories from the Bantu-speaking peoples of Africa, which include Marwe's tribe.

Kirikou and the Sorceress. DVD. Directed by Michel Ocelot. France, 1998. Distributed by ArtMattan Productions, 2000. This animated film version of an African folktale tells the story of Kirikou, a special boy who must defeat an evil sorceress.

Pritchest, Bev. *Tanzania in Pictures*. Minneapolis: Twenty-First Century Books, 2008. Learn more about modern Tanzania, the land where Marwe grew up.

Smith, Alexander McCall. *The Girl Who Married a Lion and Other Tales from Africa*. New York: Pantheon Books, 2004. This collection of more than forty stories and folktales from Africa is a wonderful introduction to the mythology and folklore of the continent.

original pencil sketch from page 7

INDEX

ABOUT THE AUTHOR AND THE ARTISTS

MARIE P. CROALL lives in Cary, North Carolina, with her loving husband and four wonderful cats. She has written for Marvel, DC, Moonstone Books, Devil's Due, and Harris Comics and is the author of the Myths & Legends books *Sinbad: Sailing into Peril*, *Ali Baba: Fooling the Forty Thieves*, and *Psyche & Eros: The Lady and the Monster*. She has also completed a self-published graphic novel and a short film.

RAY LAGO began his career as a freelance illustrator for *Reader's Digest*, Scholastic Books, and various advertising agencies. He did storyboarding, logo design, and computer graphics for NBC News, ABC News, and PBS's *McNeil/Lehrer NewsHour* before moving on to drawing and painting for Marvel and others in the comic-book industry.

CRAIG HAMILTON's work for DC's *Aquaman* led to creating graphics for bands and for movies including *Stand by Me*, *Aliens*, and *The Princess Bride*. His projects for Marvel, DC, and Vertigo include *Green Lantern*, *Legion of Super Heroes*, *Starman*, and *Fables: The Last Castle*. He lives in the historic downtown district of Macon, Georgia, with his cat, Tuesday. **Ray Snyder**, whose work as an inker includes almost every iconic comic book hero, is one of the creators of *Lazarus 5* for DC and *Dr. Strange: The Flight of Bones* for Marvel. He also lives in Macon, Georgia.